Whilst The
Angels Slept

DANIEL JEANES

Whilst The Angels Slept   Daniel Jeanes

Copyright @2014 by Daniel Jeanes

All rights reserved. No part of this publication may be reproduced, distributed, or transmitted in any form or by any means, including photocopying, recording or any other electronic or mechanical methods without prior written permission of the Author except in the case of brief quotations embodied in critical reviews and certain other noncommercial uses permitted by copyright law.

Published by Lock Publishing

Copyright © 2014 Daniel Jeanes

All rights reserved.

ISBN: 1500747505
ISBN-13: 978-1500747503

Dedicated to my wife Lauren, without your support I never could have written this novel

"What lies in our power to do, lies in our power, not to do"

Aristotle

Whilst The Angels Slept   Daniel Jeanes

CONTENTS

Prelude	Page	1
Chapter 1	Page	2
Chapter 2	Page	8
Chapter 3	Page	17
Chapter 4	Page	32
Chapter 5	Page	37
Chapter 6	Page	47
Chapter 7	Page	51
Chapter 8	Page	56
Chapter 9	Page	63
Chapter 10	Page	72
Chapter 11	Page	76
Chapter 12	Page	81
Chapter 13	Page	83
Chapter 14	Page	87
Chapter 15	Page	94
Chapter 16	Page	101
Chapter 17	Page	111
Chapter 18	Page	115
Chapter 19	Page	130
Chapter 20	Page	136
Chapter 21	Page	141
Chapter 22	Page	147
Chapter 23	Page	155
Chapter 24	Page	162
Chapter 25	Page	169
Chapter 26	Page	175
Chapter 27	Page	178
Chapter 28	Page	182
Chapter 29	Page	192
Chapter 30	Page	195
Chapter 31	Page	200
Chapter 32	Page	203
Chapter 33	Page	207
Chapter 34	Page	240

Prelude

As the withered old man surveyed the scene laid out in front of him, the carnage and destruction present was enough to take the strength from his legs, leaving him to crumble to his aging knees in a heap of disbelieve. The once indestructible city gates now lay in ruin, toppled and mangled by the Gods' unyielding wrath, a mere imitation of their former self. The once fervent and overcrowded city streets were now desolate and empty. The Emperor's palace, once a sign of the strength and perceived invincibility of the Atlantean empire, had been brought to its knees, in a similar fashion to the old man, with a similar lack of prospect for recovery. Never had the old man seen anything of such sheer rawness as what lay before him. An entire civilization destroyed; an entire Empire punished. An entire people forced to surrender in blood, sacrifice their lives before their God as payment for their crimes, or crimes they were unable to prevent.

The wail that came from the old man's throat was almost inhuman, all hope was lost, all fear and despair were now channeled into one last all-consuming act of anguish. After that, there was nothing left.

The old man could see the monstrous waves descending upon him from afar; it would not be too long before they reached him. He could feel the rush of the sea breeze, the familiar stench of the ocean, and knew all hope was long gone. He was powerless to prevent the inevitable; all he could do was stand and wait. Wait for his impending fate; wait for the ocean from whence he had come, and to whom he was returning.

1

Emperor Jhaerin the Third took once last lingering look at his throne before turning his back on it for good. There had been a time when he spent his younger days longing to sit in it, dreaming of the power and respect which would one day come when he would be named Emperor and take his place amongst his exalted ancestors. Now, the thought of it turned him to revulsion. Ever since *that* dream. Ever since the night when he went to bed ignorant, contented with his rule and the Empire he ran, and awoke with the realization of how blind he had been smacking him full force in the face, like freezing water from the Jazippi River.

Jhaerin had never been a pious man. He had taken his oaths as all boys did when they came of age, but he had never truly believed in the *Great Lord Toral*, nor in the power he supposedly possessed. Those tales were aimed at the ignorant and the foolish, who also believed in dragons and sorcerers, magicians and fairies, and other such nonsense. Now, Jhaerin knew better. Now he saw the truth of it and knew only true repentance could atone for his sins and save his people.

Walking through the Palace gates, Emperor Jhaerin was stopped by several guards, all concerned that the Emperor intended to walk into the nearby city streets without protection. All the concern in the world could not stop them from obeying a supreme command from the most powerful man in the Empire, however, and with his last official act of power, Emperor Jhaerin the Third commanded the guards present not to follow him, but to allow him to walk into the city by himself, unprotected. By the looks of shock on their faces, the Emperor knew they would instantly be on their way to inform his Head of Guards. By that time the Emperor would be gone, a stranger in the crowd, oblivious to all those who mattered, just another face in the midst of the masses, his life as unimportant as theirs.

As Jhaerin left the ancient palace, the vows he had spoken upon his coronation rang through his head, haunting him, constantly repeating without respite. The vow he had taken to protect the Empire of Atlantis, and the Atlanteans within, until the day of his death. Would he be breaking those vows this day? Jhaerin was unsure. He never had as such vowed to remain Emperor; he had vowed to protect those he served. From the dream he had received, would he not now be best-served protecting those within by warning them of the dangers that lay in the path of sin they had undertaken? To make such claims from his current position of power would ring hollow and untrue, seeing as his rule had become synonymous with corruption and the abominations that had happened during his reign. Villages pillaged, husbands murdered, woman raped, children slaughtered, and he had done nothing, turning a blind eye and believing in the piousness of his anointed High Priests, and the integrity and fortitude of his Serintinals, those charged with policing this once great Empire. All those men whose predecessors had been the noblest of all, who had made this Empire the metropolis it was.

Jhaerin was now far enough away from the Palace, on the outskirts of the city, to take a seat, in the midst of the busy crowd. Without his Empirical robes and jewels no one looked at him twice, let alone bothered speaking to him. Jhaerin put his head in his hands; a sudden weariness had come over him.

Only now did Jhaerin see the people he had trusted for what they really were, a pale comparison to their exalted predecessors, corrupted by power and greed, driven to commit monstrosities by the sole reason that they could, with no one to stop them.

I should have been the one to stop them!

Jhaerin knew he was the only one who could have stopped them, the one capable of reigning in their sprees of terror. He had been too busy enjoying his royal buffets, the pleasures of his serving girls and the joys of power that came from running an Empire, without ever taking the responsibilities that came with such a role seriously. He had made it to old age and grey hair without ever taking responsibility for his Empire's destiny, and now, in the space of his lifetime, the Empire had gone from paradise to hell on earth.

The Empire had not been in this state when his ancestors had first laid claim to the lands. It had been a true metropolis for all to behold, a garden of beauty that became the foundation for the most beautiful lands the modern world had known. It was often said

of Atlantis that once you stepped foot ashore, smelt the crisp sea air and gazed upon the greenery so lush it made every other land in the world look barren, all of the Dark Lord's Horses could not drag you off the island. A pure garden of paradise, where every man and woman could live the life of their choosing without the draconian rule of any tyrant to prohibit their will. People had once sailed from all over the world to create new lives in this great empire, this legendary land which was spoken of with fondness by all. They came from Empires and Kingdoms, which did not allow them such basic freedoms as they received in Atlantis, many former slaves, many scholars and educators travelling from lands where such skills were regarded as without use and witchcraft. They were quickly enchanted by the peace and beauty of Atlantis, bewitched by the chance of a new life in the one true garden of bliss, enticed by the prospect of living their lives without fear of persecution of enslavement.
There were too many of them!
Too many refugees, too many people looking for a new life, too many people from too many different backgrounds, creating a dangerous clash of cultures, overcrowding and hatred. The food, which had once been bountiful, much more than could be consumed, was now scarce, as was land and clean water. Too many people, too little resources. That cocktail of chaos had overcome the utopia that was Atlantis, and now, the decay of this once great civilization was evident for all to see.
This Empire which had been famed for its beauty and magnificence had become a cesspit of the vilest types of human alive, deserted by all those great men who had once claimed the island as their hope of prosperity and delight. Jhaerin knew he should have

been the one to keep the law, marshal the masses and protect *his* people, but he simply had not cared. He had been too pre-occupied with the luxuries his position afforded him, at the cost of his people. He had been convinced to allow his men to do whatever they pleased. He even allowed them to start a war with Athens, on the basis of raiding supplies from the supposedly weaker nation, although, from the news he heard on a daily basis, his men had stood no chance against their enemies vast naval power. The Greeks has defeated his men in battle and were now chasing them back across the ocean, slaughtering them by the thousands. His men were dying, far from home, because he had permitted actions without thought for consequence, trusting the men who had brought him the idea. He wondered what his advisors true motives behind invading Athens had been, not that it mattered at this point.

Jhaerin began walking again, a hundred thoughts running through his head at once. They were all based around the knowledge that he would never be able to undo his wrongs, allow the sins to which he had turned a blind eye to be reversed, or take any pleasure from the knowledge that his reign had been a good and righteous one, true to the vows he had taken upon his coronation. Until his death bed, he would know that the horrors that occurred in this Empire were his fault and that one day he would have to answer to a greater power for his sins.

Until that day, for his failings the abdicated Emperor would spend the rest of his days in poverty, preaching to whoever would listen about the dream. *That Dream*, and about the true path to repentance, the only way to avoid the dream becoming a reality and to ensure the survival of the entire Empire.

But this would not be enough. For his failings, Jhaerin would have to pay with blood and bone, a true sacrifice to the *Great Lord Toral,* the one he had doubted for so many years. Jhaerin was now out of the City, walking into the surrounding wooded area, with not one other person in sight. Kneeling down, with his left arm stretched onto a large nearby tree branch, he took a deep breath,
Blood and Bone. It must be done.
 Jhaerin unsheathed his axe, took another deep breath, his hands shaking uncontrollably, and swung, the razor sharp blade slicing through flesh and bone with the ease of a spear piercing water. The pain that came next was blinding.

2

Zanati Barina hated the market. Without question, the worst part of his day was when he had to take the little money he had earned during his mornings work laboring and, with his father Passin, walk to the local market of Baerithus. There he would peruse the fish, meats, fruits and vegetables and barter for food to take back to his mother Panitias to be cooked for dinner.
The first time he had come he had held such excitement beforehand, just at the thought of being around and bantering with the local traders, inspecting the sumptuous foods he had heard tales about. He looked forward to meeting new acquaintances who had travelled from far away exotic lands who would tell him stories of adventure. He had most of all looked forward to the stories of adventure as all young boys did. It did not take him long to realize the food was not the fresh, delicious product he had been told stories of, instead it was old and decaying, barely fit for animal consumption. The food he consumed at home was not always the nicest

tasting, but he had not realized before that his parents gave him the more edible selections. The traders barely cracked a smile upon greeting buyers, let alone offered any words of banter, and if there were any travelers with exciting stories of adventure to be told, they were keeping their mouths shut around Zanati.

The latter disappointed Zanati most of all; he had a very active imagination and, as most young boys did, a thirst for adventure and daring deeds. He often play jousted with his friends in Baerithus, the village where he lived, but with his short stature, even for his age, immature face and pale blue eyes, and the way he often yelped as though he had been thrown in a pit of fire when he took the slightest blow, there was no mistaking that he was a child trying to play a man's game. A fact which ensured he received plenty of dirty looks from the elder men in the village. Atlantis was no longer a place where one could play at battle; it would not be many more moons before the boy would be old enough to be sent for the real thing.

Being only 8, Zanati had never before seen the truth of the market before now, and so did not understand why his father was so cagey around the traders, eager to make his purchases then hastily retreat back to the relative safety of home. Zanati often heard him muttering something inaudible under his breath as they walked home; he could never work out what his father was saying but even to a child's ears it was clear the tone was always full of hate, full of resentment. Passin was a man with a short fuse; Zanati had learnt not to ask him of such things.

The first time Zanati saw the true side of the market was the third time he went. A young scholar, fresh faced and full of ideas of his own worth, had accused a trader of short-changing him for a joint of beef. At first Zanati had not realized the significance of the young scholars actions. The boy could not have been more than a few years older than him, his face still full of pimples. It was not until he noticed the look of concern upon the face of the local traders did he realize how colossal a mistake the boy had made. As he looked back from the traders horrified expressions, he saw two burly men in purple tunics grab the youth by his arms and drag him into the centre of the market. "A troublemaker huh" snarled one of the men, his voice raspy and sadistic.

"He thinks he can accuse us of stealing from him, like we need his no good coin. You probably stole it in the first place, didn't you, *academic*." The last word came out of the man's mouth as if it was made of acid, and the bitter look of disgust upon his face did little to hide the contempt he blatantly held, confusingly for Zanati.

"I think he probably did. And you know what happens to thieves, right boy?" A sadistic smile crossed the second burly man's face; Zanati was shocked by how much the man was clearly enjoying his ability to inflict terror upon the scholar. He wanted to look away, pretend this horror show was not happening in front of his very eyes, but for some reason could not. He was intoxicated by the show, incapable of turning away, equal parts curious as to what was about to happen, but unsure he wanted to know. He looked up at his father, and could see in a glance that he was facing the same dilemma.

The look of terror upon the young academics face reminded Zanati of the body paralyzing fear he saw in the young lambs on the local farms before they were slaughtered, just as they felt the sharp blade begin to slice through their neck and realized their predicament. All the self-assured cockiness which had been so evident previously had now been replaced with nothing but despair; the young man knew what fate awaited him, and was powerless to prevent it.

Why isn't anyone helping him?

"Put the noose up. A lesson needs to be made of this one. In case any of these other lying thieves start to think they can try to rob us too. They don't even realize how good we are to them." Glaring at the crowd with those words, challenging them to confront him and face his wrath, the man was clearly enjoying the show, the fear he solicited, the obedience he would no doubt get from any man present should he demand it. All Zanati could focus on was the Serpent tattoo on the man's forearms. He had heard tales since he was young about Serintinals, good men charged with protecting the Empire from evil and enforcing the Pillars of Atlantis upon anyone who tried to prevent them. He had never heard tales of wicked acts such as this one, of such men committing such evil. His *uncle* had even been a Serintinal, Zanati wondered if he was capable of such evil? He could not imagine it.

Any thoughts that this was just a threat were soon proved wrong, as the young academic was hastily dragged to the nearest tree, where a noose had been promptly erected, and against the fiercest resistance he could muster hung from the tallest branch. The look on the boys face as he at first struggled against his inevitable fate before all the fight left him, along with the air in his lungs, his face gradually turning bluer and bluer, his body going limp, had haunted Zanati even to this day. For months after, that face had been the first thing he had seen every time he closed his eyes at night, and his first thought upon awakening in the morning.

"Were those real Serintinals?" Zanati had asked his father upon the walk home.

"What do you mean, real Serintinals?" Passin had answered quizzically.

"Well, in all the stories I've been told of the Serintinals, they're always noble, heroes, good men. Those men at the market didn't seem to care about the law, that boy did nothing wrong. They killed him for nothing."

Zanati's father looked back at him with a sad look upon his face, the same look he had given him whenever he did not have enough coin to buy food for the evening, and the family would have to go without. A lean man of average height, Purias was distinctly indistinct in appearance, all except for a large zigzagging scar that went from the bottom of his neck right up to his ear on the left side of his face. A wound gained during an unprovoked attack by two drunkards many years past, when Zanati had been just a baby at his mother's breast. Passin did not speak to Zanati of that incident, pretended that it was something to be forgotten, of little significance. The scar on his neck ensured that the incident could not be forgotten with such ease, and whenever he asked his mother of it, she became very upset, to the point he had learnt to stop asking.

"The stories you were told were all true, Zanati. In my day, and the day of my father, and the days of all our ancestors, the Serintinals were a true and noble brand of warrior. Entrusted with the integrity of the Empire, they were known as *Torals* men on earth, responsible for ensuring our land remained the one true capital of the free world. Those men you saw, they're the new breed. Men willing to abuse power for their own self-gain, regardless of consequence for the citizens of this Empire. They're the reason your uncle isn't a Serintinal anymore." Passin paused, looking as though he were reluctant to continue, before taking a deep breath and proceeding, clearly pushing any doubts to one side.

"Don't pass on anything I tell you, cause they have ears everywhere, from the market to the village. It's all Emperor Jhaerins fault, the state of the Empire. His father would never have let this happen; the Empire get into such a state. But Emperor Jhaerin, he's a different breed. He doesn't care about the people like he should. All he cares about's his feasts and his whores. He's left the rest of us to cope with the monsters he's created. Those men you saw are no true Serintinals, whatever they have tattooed on them. They're nothing better than common thugs. They own all the stalls, and tell the tradesmen what they can and can't sell, and take most of the profit they make in tax. If anyone has a problem with a trader, then they have a problem with the Serintinals that are behind them, cause if the traders lose out on money then the Serintinals lose out on money. That's why they hung that man, to make an example of him and stop others doing the same. That, and the fact they're sadistic animals. That's why you're never to argue with them, no matter what they do. Do you understand?"

Zanati provided a passive nod of the head in unsure acceptance. Passin looked down at his son with a forlorn gaze. A look which told him that he understood the injustice of the situation, and even held some shame at his inability to do anything to prevent it, but that, in the end, quiet injustice was all he would be able to muster in the fight against the Serintinals and their corruption.

"I wish I didn't have to bring you along, Zanati." Passin continued with a forlorn sigh. "But you'll be a man soon, by the standards of Atlantis, and you can't hide behind your mother's knee anymore. One day you'll have a family to feed and protect, and, as much as I pray that things are better by then, I can't see it changing any time soon. You're going to have to learn to live in the Empire as it is, and that means learning to abide by the Serintinals, however hard that may be. You'll have to learn to be brave, and sometimes bravery means turning the other way, you can't fight other peoples battles in this Empire, not if you want to be able to fight your own."

Zanati looked up at his father, a look of understanding on his young face. "I know what you mean, Dad, and I'm going to be as brave as you are, I promise."

Passin smiled, giving his son a tight squeeze on his shoulder.

Zanati did not say another word for the whole journey home; he was too busy trying to process what he had heard, take it all in. All his life he had dreamed of becoming a Serintinal, a fearless warrior charged with ensuring the Pillars of Atlantis were adhered to. This news had devastated his whole reality, his dreams and prospects of who he was to become. What was he to be upon manhood now? *A Sheppard? A Fisherman?* Was he to spend the rest of his days laboring, just as he did now? It did not appeal to his sense of duty and adventure in the same way. There would be no graduation to Serintinal celebration like he had always dreamed of, there would be no hero's welcome when came back from performing some heroic deed, just a drudgingly boring life, one bound with tedium instead of honor, the same as his life was now.

He had dreaded going back the next day, having to gaze his eyes upon the boy's dead body once more and relive the horror of what he had seen. But to his shock the body was no longer there. It had been replaced by another, an older man, easily into his fortieth year, taller and more muscular than the boy, but an equally daunting image. This was made worse by the fact the man had released his bowels upon death and the area still stunk worse than the inside of one of the fishermen's boats. Zanati had tried to ask one of the other villagers what the man had done. He was a teacher in one of the local schools, but his question had been met only by sullen silence and avoidance of his gaze, followed by a harsh shove from behind from his father to keep him moving.

Since that day, many months ago now, he had seen new bodies hung on that same tree on an almost daily basis. Only rarely did he see the perpetrators being hung, and it was always for some supposed offense a Serintinal had taken, manipulating the laws to permit their actions, instead of their actions reflecting the laws currently in place. Zanati did not even see where the men were disposing of the bodies afterwards, they just seemed to have disappeared and been replaced with another. Once, back in the village, he had heard a man jest that the meat served in the market was that of the hanged men, although Zanati was beginning to wonder whether this jest had been said with unknown true words. *Had it even been a jest?* If it was not for the fact he would starve if he did not, he would have avoided eating the meat provided at the market altogether after that.

On this particular day the market was sweltering, overheated by a mass crowd that had gathered to look at the days goods and barter for what they could. The stench of stale and decaying fish was overpowering, to the point Zanati and his father both had to cover their mouths to avoid retching as they walked past several stalls. The traders always swore that their goods were freshly killed that morning, but anyone with any level of sense could tell they were lying. If not by the stench then by the way the traders could barely look at each customer as they presented them with the near rancid products. Zanatis father had told him it was not the trader's fault. Their profits were kept so low by the increasingly greedy Serintinals that they were forced to sell what they could, even if it had gone off. Zanati still found it hard to look the traders in the eye with any level of respect when his father was presented with a piece of meat that didn't look fit to be fed to the local dogs.

Father and son brought the goods they required and left the market as soon as they could, relieved to be heading back to relative safety. Neither felt the presence of eyes upon their backs as they made their exit.

3

Waking in a pool of his own vomit had become a custom for Saerphin Barina long ago. The overpowering stench of last night's wine regurgitated onto a tunic which had not been washed for going on a month was enough to make even him wretch upon awakening, causing further vomit to dredge up his throat, leaving a familiar taste. With a hazy mind and bloodshot eyes he surveyed the unfamiliar surroundings he found himself in, before groggily calling out with a cracked voice "Where in the name of Atlantis am I?" The exertion from even the simple act of speaking caused the room to spin even more, it took all Saerphins strength to keep his head upright and not vomit further.
After a few moments pause, "Torals bedchamber, where do you think you are?" came the sarcastic reply from across in the room. *At least that's a familiar voice.* Looking across the room, he now saw Jasmina, one of the Lazarias pleasure ladies, spread out

across a couch adjacent to the bed he was sprawled on.
"What are you doing over there sweetheart, plenty of room to lay with an old warrior over here." *If the room stops spinning, and if I can resist being sick.* "Yeah, but I didn't fancy sleeping in the middle of your vomit. And old warriors about right, you fell asleep before we even started last night. Don't think you're getting a Colar of your money back, I'll have a dagger in your belly before that happens." The look in the raven haired beauties eyes told Saerphin she was not joking. *Times must be tight, even for the whores.*
Saerphin chuckled as he rolled back over to try and regain some sleep, although he felt no real humor. How had his life come to this? He had once been considered by many the greatest warrior in the land, feared and revered, a champion of champions, intimidating even the most battle-hardened combatants. A true and fair warrior, he had risen to the charge of Head Serintinal, a title held by his father and his father before him, going back seven generations. Saerphin held all the family traits that made him first a worthy Serintinal and then a worthy Head Serintinal. He was strong and lean, with massive biceps, hulking shoulders and a chest which extended almost to double the size of an average man, all in proportion to his height of just over six foot, tall for an Atlantean. He had been a short child, but seemingly overnight upon his fourteenth year he had begun growing upwards, and had not stopped until his eighteenth year. Flowing blonde hair, bright as the sun, swept over a chiseled face that had been fantasized about by nigh on every maid in the Empire, a fair few of whom had enjoyed Saerphins physique closeup in his earlier days. Saerphins sharp blue eyes were always alert and vigilant. High cheekbones and

a strong, clean shaven jaw gave him the look of the perfect Atlantean, all of which when combined with his razor sharp intellect, uncompromising sense of justice and quick temper made him the quintessential Barina that the Empire had gotten to know and trust throughout the years.

The Head Serintinal was not solely a position given to the most accomplished warrior in the Empire; it was elected to the warrior most capable of ensuring the chief pillars of Atlantis were met. When a Head Serintinal retired or died, usually the latter, their predecessor was determined by battle. A vote throughout the current Serintinals for the two most eligible candidates was made, and the two chosen warriors would battle it out, to the death, for the honor of the post.

When first introduced the battle had just been until one man had submitted but too many times men not willing to do whatever was necessary within the position had succeeded against weaker opponents. The winner's inabilities only becoming evident once they held the position. To the death was the only way to ensure any man willing to fight for the position was truly dedicated to all the responsibilities involved. To Saerphins knowledge no man had ever argued with that theory, although plenty had backed out once selected, which was their right. If you were willing to die to win the position, you would be willing to die to keep it, if not then you were not. It was as simple as that. Saerphin thought back to the day he won the post.

There had never been any question in Saerphin's mind when his predecessor, Marxillian, had died that he would be one of the chosen candidates, and there was also no surprise when his opponent, Julias, was also chosen. A smaller man than Saerphin, Julias made up for his size inadequacies with speed and cunning, traits of a great warrior. Saerphin had known the man since he was a child; they had broken bread, played in the woods and swam as children, kept the citizens of Atlantis safe side by side. But all that was in the past, Saerphin knew that Julias would show him no mercy, so the only way to survive was to not show any back.

The battle was fought on a rare rainy day. The clouds hanging overhead darkened the skies, and an uncompromising breeze swept through the Empire, sending chills down even the most battle-hardened of the thousands who came to spectate. As soon as the horn was blown, Julias was upon him, lurking safely out of distance before lunging elegantly towards him, swinging precisely, dancing the dance he had learnt so long ago, the dance he had learnt alongside Saerphin. But the problem Julias faced was that Saerphin knew the dance all too well, knew every move, every sway, every faint and every step. Julias swarmed towards Saerphin, swinging his sword ferociously with his right hand, Saerphin blocked and countered; his blade narrowly missing Julias's neck. Now Saerphin was off guard, Julias tried to take advantage, swinging low, but Saerphin managed to hop out of the way of the subtle low swing, the edge of the sword inches from his thigh muscles. The dance continued, for how long Saerphin could not remember, he had been too much in his own zone. One man attacked, one man countered. Each man unable to outwit the other, a stalemate created by familiarity yet the crowd mesmerized by the performance, unable to look away, wowing at every blow, every near miss, waiting for that one moment, that one mistake, when they would have their champion.

Both men stopped to catch their breath, now circling one another, appraising the other man's next move. Saerphin had the considerable size advantage, but Julias had swiftness, cunning and an unwavering belief in winning at all costs which the rest of the Empire did not believe that Saerphin possessed. Saerphin later learnt that despite his size advantage, the majority of the bets had been against him that day. This was not because it was doubted he was the better fighter, but because it was thought his well known moral compass would not allow him to kill a friend,

Julias was the first to move again, this time feinting to cut inside to Saerphins right before spinning three hundred and sixty degrees and swinging wildly at Saerphins left, putting his full power and momentum behind the manouvre. The move might have worked perfectly, should have worked perfectly, had it not been for the fact that Saerphin had seen him do it too many times before, albeit usually with a wooden sword. He had been expecting the move at some point, he knew Julias always pulled it out when desperate, and always swung too wildly when attempting it, assuming he had tricked his opponent and would have a clean shot. The look in his eyes was of sheer surprise and terror when he did not make contact. His sword flew in front of Saerphin, who taking a step back, felt the gush of air as the blade glided harmlessly past his body. and who now had Julias completely defenseless to his impending attack. Julias was unable to halt the momentum which continued to take his sword across his body, he desperately tried planting his feet to stop the momentum carrying his whole body with it, just about succeeding with a slight stumble. It would take but a second to bring his sword back across, but both men knew that would be a second too late. Saerphin had been dreading this moment, the moment he would have to kill his friend, but in actuality it came to him a lot easier than expected, the guilt not appearing until later days. With one swift, clinical movement, his sword rammed firmly into his friend, colleague and opponent's throat, deep enough so that the blade appeared the other side, a deep, crimson seeping underneath the blade from the man's wound, the way water seeps from a sinking boat. Saerphin caught a flicker of acceptance in the eyes of his friend, before nothing, emptiness. And to the victor went the spoils.

After going through so much to claim the position, Saerphin truly believed in offering his all to his people, and in such had truly believed in the morals and fortitude of those that ruled in the great Empire. That had been a long time ago. There had been a single moment when he had realized all he had worked for had been for nothing, a moment of clarity in which his faith in the protectors of the once great society had been lost forever. There had, as with most losses of faith, been a gradual decline in belief, but it was brought to a head one day by an act of such evil Saerphin shuddered whenever he thought about it, which even now was on a daily basis.

Saerphin could still see her eyes as she lay in front of him, full of terror and confusion. What they had done to her had been horrific; her wounds so festered even the local dogs had avoided trying to eat what remained of her, although clearly by the bite wounds up and down her legs some at least had tried. Saerphin had not seen her lying in a ditch at the side of the forest, or even heard her whimpers, which by the time he came across her were no louder than those of a child. What had alerted him to her presence had been the stench, gangrene and sweat mixing to create a smell so foul he would remember it until the end of his days. At times when he awoke in a cold sweat during the night, he could swear that that stench was still imposed upon his nose. Upon inspection, Saerphin had found her, naked and alone, terrified and mutilated. What had been done to her Saerphin truly believed no human of this earth could have commissioned, yet clearly his faith in mankind had been misplaced. His own people had done this.

Upon trying to speak to the girl, words of comfort and words aimed at discovering who had committed this monstrosity, only two words were croaked from her mouth, so slowly and with such effort it pained Saerphin even to hear them. "Kill….me!" When Saerphin was having his nightmares, remembering that terrible day, it was that moment that always came foremost in his mind. Haunting him, forcing him to relive what he to this day prayed he would be permitted to forget, but which had been permanently etched upon his memory, as though a tattooist from one of the far exotic lands had imprinted it on the insides of his eyelids, unrelenting, uncompromising, unforgettable.

The woman's piercing green eyes, probably once pretty, were now drooping and withdrawn. Her thick lips, which would once have been described as luscious, were now cracked and broken, probably largely from being bitten down upon to distract herself during the most excruciating and unbearable parts of her torture. Her olive skin, which would once have been glowing in the healthy manner Atlantean skin did, was caked in mud and other such matter, masking how pale her skin had become during her ordeal. Her head was full of remnants of what may once have been beautiful thick dark hair, but which had been hacked off and left her with mere wisps covering her skull, like that of a babe. What lay before him was no more than the empty shell of what was once a human being, a citizen of this great Empire which he had vowed to protect, a promise which he had clearly failed to deliver.

Saerphin knew there was just one thing he could do to end this woman's suffering, and bring her to a deserved eternal peace. Without another word, he unsheathed the sharp blade he stored in his left boot, and with one precise slice across the woman's throat ended all her pain, her blood splattering over his eyes and mouth. It had not been a hard decision, and the look of gratitude in the dying woman's eyes as he drew the blade close told him more than even her words had of her wishes. Saerphin wished he saw that look in his nightmares, the look of appreciation that told him he had done the right thing, but all he was permitted to see was the feral look in her eyes as he first came across her. He would never forget that face.

As Head Serintinal, Saerphin vowed that whoever committed this act would be brought to justice, and that that justice would be located at the end of his sword. The corpse bore a host of unique scars and brands, some fresh, some slightly older, all distinctive; they had clearly taken their time with her enjoyed the torture and her agony. Strange angles and foreign letters, forged so deep into the woman's skin they had become a part of her, were etched all the way from her ankles to her forehead. Saerphin had never seen these marks before and had no concept of their significance. The only brands he had ever seen had been on former slaves from across the seas, horrific burns of various insignias that had once signified the slave masters ownership of that person. But the act of slavery had always been banned in Atlantis, each man and woman seen as equal and free to follow their own path in life. That had clearly not been the case here.

To uncover the truth of the situation, and determine who to lay the blame for the monstrosity in front of him with, Saerphin knew he had to take the body to the Royal Courts, to lay the horrific corpse in front of the Magistrates charged with justice within the Empire. There he would seek what answers he could, demand an investigation, identify the victim, inform her family, seek a culprit and extract revenge.

What I would have given to have extracted revenge.

Upon Saerphin entering the courts with the mutilated corpse, each man present had feigned shock and fury, indignation that this had been allowed to happen within their great metropolis. But in the end, it was clear the pledge he was bringing forth to uncover the twisted perpetrator or perpetrators and bring them to justice was destined for failure. There had been a time when Head Serintinal had been the most-respected position within the Empire, a figure whose words were adhered to regardless of anything else and who had the authority to launch enquiries based on his own whims, without argument. This was no longer the case. Every man who expressed their disgust at the mutilated corpse that lay in front of them also articulated various reasons why they could not assist in the matter of finding the guilty party.

Eventually, after nearly an hour of debate with some of the most important men within the Empire, one of the young magistrates, Bartholomew, gently placed an arm around Saerphins' hip and led him to a vacant corner of the room.

"I fear you do not understand the situation you have uncovered." The man had a sweet, quiet voice, and spoke with hushed words. He was constantly looking

over his shoulder, at some apparent threat unknown to Saerphin. He was clearly unwilling to allow this conversation to be carried across the room, and hesitant to help Saerphin at all, but also unwilling to not give answers where he could. Torn between two forces, he was doing what he could to pacify both.
I bite harder than them; I can assure you!
Saerphin did not have time for this man's paranoia, nor his gentle approach. "I fear you do not understand. I am Head Serintinal. I made a pledge to protect the people of this Empire, to uphold the Pillars of Atlantis. And now, when I've found a body such as this, you expect me just to forget about it, leave it for the wolves. What do I not understand? Tell me, make me understand what I clearly do not!" Saerphins voice was gradually getting louder; he could not care less about the phantom threat in the room, and even hoped this threat would show the fortitude to face him. As his temper rose his sword hand began to get twitchy, his blood began to boil, his adrenaline was pumping, he was eager for confrontation, desperate for it, regardless of the consequences.
Bartholomew looked sheepishly back at Saerphin, his discomfort evident by the rising redness in his face. The seasoned warrior was beginning to wonder why the other magistrates had left this rookie to bring him this news, were they spineless or did they just not respect his position anymore?
"Look, we all respect you as a great warrior, but there are things afoot that we, and you, can do nothing about. I would love nothing more than to allow you to seek vengeance, find these monsters, but the men who committed this act are...protected..shall we say." The young magistrate awkwardly shifted his feet before continuing. Saerphin could tell he was becoming gradually more weary of his reactions,

trying to choose words that would not bring anger. "From higher powers, those who hold the true power in the Empire." Bartholomew let those last words sink in for a few seconds, although he could not help but flinch at the look of anger that crossed Saerphins face as he spoke them, half expecting the great man to lash out, with fist or sword.

"Protected?" Saerphin growled. "What in the name of Atlantis do you mean protected?" Saerphin was no longer in control of his voice; he was now on the verge of shouting right into the young magistrates face, his nose a mere few inches away. "Who are they protected by? Maybe they're who I should be speaking too. Perhaps they would like to meet face to face, sword in hand." Saerphins face had begun to turn a deep shade of red, with the temples on his forehead throbbing rapidly; his breathing was fast and heavy, spittle uncontrollably flying from his mouth all over Bartholomew's pale startled face. The young magistrate looked like he would rather be anywhere in the world but there at that moment.

"Men who hold the power." Bartholomew stuttered. "Men you do not want to cross. You must believe me; I do not wish harm to come to you. Please, just leave this be Saerphin. It would be so much easier for everyone."

"You've as much chance of growing breasts and joining one of the bleeding brothels. Now tell me, who are they and who's protecting them?" Every eye in the room was now on the two men, although everyone was too far away to hear anyone but Saerphin, whose voice was now so loud everyone else in the room may as well have been standing next to him. No other man present had the bravery to come closer and join the conversation, so they gawped from afar, vicariously

embracing the situation young Bartholomew found himself in,
Cowards.

By this point the young man was sweating profusely, thick beads running from his forehead and rolling slowly over his face, dribbling from his nose and cheeks down to his neck. His speech had become stuttered, his pitch high and squeaky, like that of a child pre-puberty. "The men are known as...Saritins Acolytes..." Bartholomew whispered the name, as though it held the power to cause him to burst into flames, "and as I said they are not men to be crossed. They have friends, friends in the palace. Friends who allow them to exist, and allow them to do what they must do. The girl, she was a sacrifice, to *Saritin*, to their *Dark Lord.*"

"I know who *Saritin* is." Saerphin knew the magistrates and academics viewed his type as brutes and imbeciles, but he was in no mood to play the part.

"Well, they believe that one day he will walk on earth, and that until that day they must do his bidding, to become allies so that he will elevate them upon his arrival, elevate them to great power. The palace, I do not know who has befriended them, but we've been made aware that these Acolytes are not to be sought after. We don't even know who they are. All we know is that they're...they're untouchable. If you attempt to go after them...we'll be forced to strip you of all duties. You and your family will be prosecuted for dereliction of duty...it won't just be you that's hurt, and it will get very ugly Saerphin, I promise you. They won't show any mercy. We have no choice."

Saerphin looked down at the young man with pure, undisguised disgust, before raising his head and slowly looking around the room, his gaze lingering on each man and fixing them with a harsh look of contempt before moving his stare to the next man. "So this is the way of it. Me, a man sworn to bring justice to the people of Atlantis. You, the men sworn to uphold justice and ensure fairness. Both of us, sworn to uphold the Pillars of Atlantis. And, seemingly, neither of us about to do it. Me, unable. You, unwilling. Well, I can tell you now, I will not hold an empty position, and I will not pay lip-service to any Emperor that allows…that allows THIS," Saerphin pointed to the corpse laid in the middle of the floor, "This…MONSTROSITY to take place un-avenged." With one last look across the room, Saerphin released the buckle which held his sword and threw it at the feet of Bartholomew, to gasps of shock throughout the room. He did not look back as he stormed out of the room, shoving aside any man who stood in his way.

That had been some eight months previous or there about. Saerphin could not state an exact time frame, as he had spent a considerable amount of his time since either in a drink induced slumber or awake, but too intoxicated to worry about such things as time, let alone unnecessary tasks such as bathing, shaving or keeping himself properly nourished. As often as not, largely due to a lack of coin, he replaced food for drink, preferring to spend his nights with wine to keep the memories away instead of food to dissipate his hunger pangs. He could cope with the hunger pains; he could not cope with the memories.

The money he did get was gained providing security for local politicians and men of commerce, working as an armed guard whenever they conducted liaisons in the less safe areas of the Empire. They were usually unethical and even illegal business dealings, but at least they paid half decent coin, enough for a flagon of wine and potentially a lady for the night at least.

The ladies always took the pain away, for as long as he could afford them for at least.

It had been a worry at first that he might be recognized, that stories would be released of how the great Saerphin, greatest of the Serintinals, was now hiring his sword to anyone with sufficient coin. He did not care from his own point of view, but the thought of bringing shame to his family, of bringing embarrassment to the seven good men, good Barinas who had held the position of Head Serintinal previous to him, was painful in itself. However, it became clear soon enough that no one even looked twice at him. Even if they did, whilst his natural physique would tell them he was at one point a warrior, they would not expect the bearded man reeking of wine, body odour and vomit to be the once greatest warrior in the Empire, the legendary Saerphin.

Only in moments of clarity such as this one, usually after a heavy night of drinking and whoring, did Saerphin take stock of his life and contemplate how far he had fallen. Not once had he ever regretted his actions in bringing the corpse to court, but he did regret his decision to walk out near enough every day, an act of petulance which he could not undo. He had always been hot-headed, with a penchant for reacting to situations before he had properly considered the consequence of his actions, but this time he had made a mistake of enormous repercussions. Now, instead of being able to continue to search for the girl's torturers from a position of power, and go after these Acolytes with all the might of the Serintinals, he was a man on his own, powerless and impotent to exact any revenge.

He had expected his men to follow his suit when they discovered his actions, to throw down their swords and walk with him, force the courts and the Palace to reconsider. They would give him their blessings to pursue the perpetrators with all his power, without repercussions for his family, but it did not take long for him to realize how wrong that assumption had been. Once he had walked, disrespected the role he had been blessed with, he knew he would never get it back. Only after he had relinquished his position and power did Saerphin see the truth of the men who he had trusted with his reign, who he would have trusted with his life. The men who acted righteous and fair in his presence were the opposite in the markets of the Empire, sadistic and power hungry, greedy and self motivated. He had been blind to their actions, and now was powerless to bring them to heel.

With all these thoughts running through his head, Saerphin realized that sleep would not come, so got up and walked to the door. His shame would not enable him to bring himself to look at the whore laid out on the bed before quietly slipping out onto the Baerithus streets. The wine merchants were calling.

4

The scent within the chamber was a lustrous mix of lavender and vanilla, beautifully entwined to compose a sweet, fresh aroma, lingering in the nostrils, intoxicating to all who entered. However, in contrast the five aged men within the room were anything but sweet and fresh, in everything but soul. They were men pure of heart, but old of body, men who had helped shape the empire into what it was, men who had dedicated their entire lives to preserving this paradise on earth, the great metropolis that was the Empire of Atlantis.

To the people of the empire they were barely known at all, but those who did know of them knew them as the "The Angels of Atlantis," wise men who as a fraternity had existed for over four hundred years. They held the sole purpose of acting as a moral compass for those within the Empire, a light in the darkness to guide the people's souls to the eternal paradise of the afterlife as the *Great Lord Torals* guardians on earth.

To become an Angel, a man had to spend a minimum of thirty years unblemished service to *Toral*, devout and uncompromised by the temptations of ordinary men. Women, violence, gluttony, opium's designed to alter one's mindset, all were put aside when a man took the vows of Maral, and only by keeping these temptations separate from their lives could a Marale hope to elevate to the position of Angel. Even violence against unholy men was not permitted, for in the end even men of no faith, or even worse those men who worshipped the *Dark Lord Saritin*, would, in due course, be held to account when their death day came. There they would be forced to account for their sins in the chamber of the *Great Lord Toral*. Although violence by men outside the fraternity in the name of *Toral* was permitted to be supported when necessary.

On this day, each man present exhibited a grave look upon their withered face. They had fought their whole lives for good. They had dedicated the best parts of their adulthood to the fight against evil, serving as a guide to the morally blind, but it seemed their crutch had been broken in two, snapped by a force too great for them to resist, as though a tiger's monstrous teeth had crashed through, leaving their abilities broken and ineffective. Each man stared into the flames, and each man saw the same vision. Hell upon earth. Waves, higher than the tallest trees the empire had to offer, crashing through stone buildings as though they were made of paper. Children running amuck, trampled by fleeing adults in scenes of panic, a mistimed harmony of shrill screams, a scramble of peoples horrific demise, death taking its prizes indiscriminate of age or gender. The deserving and the undeserving perished with equal frequency; no one was safe from this deadly destruction.

One of the men could stand the images no more, and carefully doused the flames which projected the images with a nearby bucket of water, methodically ensuring each ember had been sufficiently soaked. None of the men spoke for a long moment of time, each man taking in what they had just seen, trying with all their will to comprehend the vision and its repercussions. Eventually Siphorious, the eldest of the men spoke, with long, drawn out breaths.

"What we just saw was horrific. It was catastrophic. Until we saw these images, it would have been unimaginable. But now, my friends, we have seen the destiny the *Great Lord Toral* has determined fit for our Empire. For too long, our people have failed to follow the guidelines that we have set out. That *He* set out. They have not adhered to the messages sent from above. They have ignored our pleas for peace, for tranquility. Our *Great Lord Toral* is angry with us, and I for one do not blame him." The old man had to pause for a second to catch his breath; it was clear to each man present that the gravity of the situation, as much as the length of time speaking, had taken their toll on him. Finally, he continued.

"My friends, the *Great Lord Toral* came to me in a dream. He brought me the visions you saw in front of you today. And he told me why such venom was to be released upon our world. Evil has taken hold, wrapped its vicious presence around this great Empire and strangled it until our people cannot comprehend His glory. They have lost their consciences and with it all sense of morality. The *Great Lord Toral* has given us one last chance for repentance, one final shot at saving our people from this fate." Again, the old man paused for breath; his speech was becoming slower, his chest wheezing loudly due to the exertion.

"There is to be an act committed within the near future. It will be an act so evil *Toral* would not bring its details into my vision. My brothers, if this act is permitted to occur, all hope is lost. The vision you saw in front of you will be destined to become a reality, and all prayers for salvation will not be met, regardless of how piously any man within the Empire is willing to prey." The elderly man once again stopped for respite, and to gauge the reaction of his peers. Although each man was elderly, he could see the fight was still within them. These were proud men, determined men, men more than capable of committing to the work required of them.

"What would the *Great Lord Toral* have us do, my friend. We are His to command." The man who spoke had only a few remaining soft wisps of white hair covering a head covered with large liver spots. Bushy white eyebrows almost covered his bright, emerald eyes, and in his younger days he might have been strong, although now his body had decayed to a mere shell, stooped and weltering.

"Tarinthium, we will do what we can, as I know you are all willing to do. This is not a large Empire, but even so, there are frankly too many men and women to even contemplate trying to reach each one. Too many times we have released our prophecies to the public. And every time we have been met with ignorance and denial. Even now, you can feel the weather changing. The cold is coming, and with it the storms that may cause our end of days."

"My brothers, we are old, and we are weak. But we are not powerless. The *Great Lord Toral* has set me forth a plan, which I will set in motion. He has sent us an Angel, a *true* and *righteous* Angel, a man capable of being our savior, our hero in our darkest hour. I know what I must do, and if it works, the Empire shall be saved. If it doesn't, then all is lost. But what we must do, each day, we must pray. We must pray to the *Great Lord Toral* for the forgiveness our people will seek. Should he require our bodies for sacrifice, we will provide them to him. And if this act of evil should still occur, then our people will know the wrath of their master, but we will pray that he is merciful in the end. My friends, come kneel with me, let us pray."

5

"Gone? What do you mean gone?" Head Priest Purias bellowed loudly at the young serving girl Andrea. Having drunk a copious amount of wine the previous evening, as he did most evenings, Purias was unsure whether he had heard the girl correctly. "When you say Emperor Jhaerin has gone, tell us exactly what you mean? And be precise girl, I don't have time to waste with tall tales, don't think I'll hesitate to have the skin whipped off your back if you leave anything out. I did it to a boy the same age as you last week for much less."
The freckle-faced girl stuttered "well…I…I…I was sent to tell you that….the E..E..Emperor isn't in his bedchamber….he's left a note…I have it if you like…it says he's left, and he's not coming back."
The Head Priest frowned. A heavy set man by nature made heavier by excessive drinking and feasting, he reminded Andrea of the Walruses she had heard the travelling men speak of, even down to the scruffy dark whiskers which covered his cheeks and chin. The look on his face right now was frighteningly

reminiscent of one of the pictures she had seen drawn of the creatures from the travelers who would pass through his village. Andrea could not remember whether the beasts feasted on human flesh although she counted that lack of knowledge a blessing. Purias snatched the letter from her hand, before shoving her in the direction of the door "Out with you girl! Don't you have some work to be doing?" Andrea was relieved to be leaving the drunkard's company, as well as to be away from the overwhelming stench of wine on the man's breath. As she walked through the doors, she wondered whether she could get drunk just from breathing it in.

After reading through the words several times to ensuring he had read each correctly, Purias handed the letter to his companion, and fellow drunk, Mentithius, who also carefully read through the letter, squinting when his vision blurred from the wine. The two Priests stared at each other in shocked bewilderment. "Well I'll be, I didn't see this coming" snorted Mentithius. More wily and sinewy than Purias, but with an equally vein ridden nose, he was often compared in appearance to a ferret, although never to his face. As Purias's right hand man, he was equally feared throughout the palace, and equally keen on abusing the power which came with his elevated position.

Purias chuckled heartily. "So the old man finally lost his bottle huh, decided he'd rather live with the rats and peasants than in his fancy palace. I always knew there was something wrong with that one. Never had the bottle his father had. Well, at least his whelp should be just as receptive as to how to run an Empire. The best Emperors are the ones who know when to shut their over-indulged mouths up and do as they're told," Purias snorted. He was gradually becoming excited by the development.

"Tinithius, aye, give the boy his toys to play with, and he couldn't care less what happens to the rest of the realm." Mentithius replied.

"You know what; I'm sensing an opportunity here." The look on Purias's face was one the whole realm had seen before, usually when he was thinking up some cunning plan to con some unsuspecting victim at a card game or demand some peasants' daughter for the night. "With the old Emperor off playing savior, and the new Emperor too young to be of any use to anyone, the Empires going to need someone to run it, even more than before. Someone to choose the laws, decide who has to pay extra levies, whose young daughters should become servant girls in the palace chambers? We could do with some nice young ladies around here; I think the current lot are pretty much at their expiry date."

"Aye, smell like they are. Still, we gotta play this careful. We look too obvious we're trying to take the Emperor's power; them advisors around him around gonna start asking questions. We don't want to be on the wrong side of them if we can avoid it"

"They can ask all the question they want. They ask the wrongs once and I'll have their head on a pike. They may think they run this Empire, but let me tell you, it was our ancestors who built it, and it's us that's keeping it in line." Purias banged his fist on the table to make his point. He had a short fuse when he was sober, when he had a drink in his system he was as unpredictable as a man could be, as many men in the Empire had discovered to their detriment.

"The Emperor thinks he can surround himself with some Greek exile bastards and trust them to advise him on how to run this Empire, he's got another thing coming. I don't trust them Greeks, not one bit. They'll hand our lands over to their countrymen in a heartbeat if we give them a chance. They'll turn our ships around, bring them back here, and tell us to roll over and have our bellies tickled whilst they rape and pillage our lands. Without us, the Empire would have fallen to ruin before it began, or them foreigners would have come smashing through our doors and added us to their lands. Aye, a lot to thank us for has this Empire, and they best not forget it."

Mentithius smiled; a sly smile that may have been mistaken by Purias as in agreement with the statement he had made, although in truth Mentithius was purely amused by the older man's guile. He knew as well as Purias did that this was not about what was rightfully theirs, any more than it was about what was best for the people of the Empire. This was about man doing what man did best since the dawn of time, self-preservation and looking after one's own self-interest. With Emperor Jhaerin self-dethroned, the Empires unofficial rule was theirs for the taking, and both men knew it.

"My brothers, I trust you are well." Both men were startled by the sudden emergence of Avyon's soft voice, so delicate it was almost a whisper, to be overpowered by the most gentle of summer breezes. The most senior of all priests in Atlantis, in truth there was nothing to fear at all with Avyon, he was as timid as they came. Due to his seniority, he had been offered the position of Head Priest, before even Purias's predecessor. Avyon had turned it down as he felt he was better positioned helping the people of the Empire in his current role, providing spiritual relief and guidance, without the added politics which came from the elevated position. With hair white as a dove, a kindly face and pleasant features, Avyon had often been called Grandfather by his fellow priests, and his gentle nature and unflinching devotion to the *Great Lord Toral* lent itself further to his kind old man image.

"Avyon, what in the name of Toral are you doing creeping up on us like that? You'll give us a heart attack." Purias all but spat the words, more enraged by the fact he had not been alert to the man's presence than that he had crept up upon them unawares. *Must be the wine.*

"My apologies if I startled you, I was just passing by and saw you were in conversation. I guess I don't really need to ask what the conversation topic is. What a shock, an abdicated Emperor. Who but the *Great Lord Toral* saw that coming?"

"Aye, if he saw that coming why didn't he warn us, we could've made preparations. Caught us from behind in a sea storm this did. He who's so powerful, didn't see this coming did he, or wasn't paying any attention to us down here." Mentithius spoke each word with a smirk, he knew Avyon would fall for the bait.

"Good sir, I ask that you do not make comedy at our *Great Lords* expense. One day He will be making judgment upon you, and when that day comes, I will pray for your soul. Until then, trust that it is wise to hold your tongue in such matters." When Avyon spoke, his face glowed with an understated conviction. He was not an animated speaker, and with his modest demeanor and hushed voice he would never match the preachers that roamed the markets throughout the Empire in magnetism, but what Avyon lacked in charisma he made up in sincerity and earnestness. He was a man devoted to his cause, unwaveringly loyal to his god. However, the two men present had never cared about the olds mans devotions or kindness, and Mentithius at least had gone a long way past caring whether he was aware of their lack of regard for him.

"Old man, your God, our God, all that matters is that we have no Emperor. Think of that when you're saying your next prayers."

"What I think Mentithius means to say" Purias intersected hastily," is that the boy Tinithius now has an important role to fill, and that means we've got a coronation to plan. I have never seen one, let alone planned one, but what I can tell you is that it needs to be big. Spectacular. So awe-inspiring, the people will talk of it for years." *And talk of the trustworthiness of good old Purias, who planned it all.* "No expense shall be spared. The finest fish from the ocean, the primest meat from the best farmers, the best wine the Empire has to offer. Whatever the cost, we'll pay it." *If it costs the crown that will sit atop Tinithius's head, so be it.* "I'm going to give you a list of supplies we need, your job is to make sure we have them all. It will not do for anything to not be right on the day, remember that. I have my full trust in you." Purias gave the old man a reassuring smile, although the lack of sincerity could not have been hard to notice. Purias was not a man who often smiled, so when he did it usually looked lopsided and forced, as though he had wooden instruments on the inside of his plump cheekbones, pushing outward. The large red wine stains on his teeth did little more to lend to his attempts at sincerity.

"I'll do my best, but need I remind you the Empire is not exactly awash with capital, nor food for that matter. Do you want the new Emperor starting the same as the old, by holding lavish parties completely oblivious to the suffering of his people? Do you not feel that a more subdued coronation, perhaps without excess food and such copious amounts of wine as usual, may carry young Tinithius more favor than the extravagant feasts that have become the norm with the old regime? I fear this public backlash may be the reason for Emperor Jhaerins departure, may the *Great Lord* grant him mercy, do you want that same pressure added to the shoulders of our new Emperor? Such pressure on such young shoulders may crack them before they can flourish into the shoulders that carry this Empire back to greatness."

To Hell with our new Emperor, and the pressure on his shoulders. So long as he keeps his mouth shut and allows me to control him like I controlled his father, he can have the pressure of Chiawanga on his shoulders for all I care. Let it break his body like I intend to break his will.

Avyon had an annoying habit of talking down to people, even those who were technically his superiors, feeling he was superior due to his age and his undoubted piousness. The condescending tone in his voice made Purias want to grab him by the throat and smash his head into the concrete floor. However, Purias knew that Avyon was potentially a key ally, and so approached the subject with a forced subtly which displayed his ability to be tactful when required, no matter how much it gave him a headache. He would have to teach Mentithius his skills of diplomacy.

"Avyon, I understand your concerns, I truly do. We all pray for Jhaerin, from the bottom of our hearts, and sincerely hope he has found peace where ever he may be. He was a good man, but let us not forget, he *has* abandoned us. Abandoned his people, his Empire, his son even. All this talk of famine, of prophecies, of war, people, have forgotten their objectives. We are still the most powerful Empire in the world, the most advanced, and the most civilized. If you hear differently, you must be getting wrong information from the outside." *And when I find out whose providing you that information, I'll have their guts on my dinner table.*

"Now, as we are still the most powerful, and greatest Empire this world has ever known, do you not feel we need a strong Emperor? Someone with the balls and guile to drive us towards becoming greater? How can you have a great Emperor who's afraid to throw a lavish feast for his own coronation? The people will feel him weak, and his rule will count for naught. It may seem over the top to you, as it does to me also, but you must look at the bigger picture." *The picture which sees me at the head of the table, with my hands behind Tinithius, controlling him like the puppet masters control the puppets at the carnivals.*

"We're fighting for something greater, and sometimes to solidify the image of a great Emperor, coin has to be spent. It's always been that way I'm afraid."

Mentithius was holding back a grin; he had forgotten exactly how good a liar Purias could be. When required, the Head Priest could sell lamb to the farmers, water to the fisherman, books on homosexuality to the Greeks. This trait had been a big reason behind him being elected Head Priest in the first place, this and the quick turn of temper behind closed doors which had intimidated several electors into changing votes when the silver tongue treatment had not worked. However, the look on Avyons face said that the pious old man was not buying this particular tale, and Mentithius wondered whether subtlety would go out the window and be replaced by rage here.

"I understand what you're saying, but the people are discontented." Avyon said. "They feel we're taking too much of their taxes, and that they're not getting enough back. Banquets like the one we're planning are a slap in the face to a poor family who barely have

enough to feed their family at night, and the Serintinals out there don't help matters. Some of the stories I've heard, I'm not even going to repeat them, let's just say they're disgusting. If these people are who are meant to be keeping the Empire civilized, I'd say we're a long way off that."
Civilized? Who said anything about the Serintinals making the Empire more civilized? They're there to make sure we get our taxes. How they do that, I couldn't care less.
"I understand fully, my friend, the people aren't happy. But a new Emperor will soon put an end to that. The people love a new ruler, someone to come in and be aspired to. The boy may just be twelve years of age, but it's our job to make him loved, to make him the type of leader the people will follow to the end of the earth." *And if they don't, as long as they keep paying their taxes, and I'm still Head Priest, they can be as unhappy as they want.* "And this business about the Serintinals. They're the protectors of the Empire, do you really think they would commit acts such of these? I've heard similar tales myself, and when I've investigated they always turned out to be false." *That's at least half true. I've heard plenty of stories, but never bothered investigating. If the people think the Serintinals are bad now, wait to see what they're like if this doesn't go to plan.* "My brother, I'm afraid my decision is final. The feast shall be one the Empire will never forget, and solidify our new Emperor Tinithius in the realm of truly great Emperor, to successfully rule this Empire for years to come. Now I think we've all got plenty to be getting on with; these are exciting times. But first, let us pray."
Avyon bowed to his knees to say his prayers, a look of discontent still evident on his face for his two companions to see. Just before Purias bowed his

head, he glanced through the large glass windows ahead. He could have sworn he saw the clouds begin to turn a little bit darker.

6

The sun above was repressive and unbearable, constantly beating onto the ships hull and instantly zapping the fatigue of anyone left exposed to it for too long. For several members of the Atlantean Empirical Fleets second ship, the same as the other ships in the fleet, the sun was upon them without respite, causing several men to pass out already. There was no time to provide medical assistance for these men, the ones who were still alive were rolled into the few areas of shade there were to recover, the ones who did not appear to still be breathing were rolled off the ship to their watery grave below. Less men, less weight, the more chance they had of out running the monstrous collage of Greek warships currently chasing them back west.

"They're catching up; we need to lose more weight!" The ship's Captain, Cronias, yelled. A tall, well-built man, with authority to spare, everyone paid attention when he spoke, regardless of the situation. "Throw the potatoes over, and any of the other heavy foods. We need to lose anything unnecessary." The

Captain looked around and spotted a recently passed out sailor. "Try and wake him up if he doesn't, chuck him. Belly like that, he's probably the one slowing us down."

"Yes sir." Several of the men replied, knowing better than to object to their commanders instruction. Two of the men proceeded to the food storeroom just below the hull, whilst another prodded the man to see if he was still alive.

"Throw the potatoes over, we haven't eaten in well over a day." Gurain grumbled. "If we keep going this way, we won't have enough energy nor enough people to get us back to Atlantis."

"I know, if I don't eat something soon I think I'm going to pass out." Janithia replied. "I don't want to be kicked off the side of the ship; I can't swim."

Gurain chuckled. "Then why did you join the Empirical Fleet?"

Janithia shrugged. "At the time it didn't look like we were going to be at war, so I didn't think I'd ever be in this situation. Plus, I kinda just imagined I'd learn."

The two men hauled the bags of potatoes, apples and various other fruits to the deck, before proceeding to throw them overboard. Despite their almost crippling hunger, neither man took the opportunity to take a bite of the food they were throwing away, knowing the consequences if Captain Cronias discovered them. As both Captain and Commander, he was all powerful, and ruled with an iron fist. Eating the food without permission, even if it were about to be thrown overboard, would be stealing, and they both knew they would be following the food overboard if they were caught doing that.

He'd probably begrudge us the extra weight we put in our bellies from the food as well; Gurain thought.

Both men retook their places at the oars and proceeded to row as fast and as hard as they could, the familiar ache returning to their shoulders as soon as their oars struck the water.
It wasn't supposed to be like this.
When Gurain had joined the Atlantean Empirical Fleet, he had done so because he was told they were the greatest in the world. He would travel to distant lands, see adventures, win great battles, rule supreme over the enemies of his great Empire.
No-one had ever said anything about losing.
No-one said anything about the possibility that they would be being chased back across the ocean with their tails between their legs, by boats full of Greek warriors, driven by some of the most resilient slaves around. The type of slaves that had been born and bred with an oar in their hands. Even with the extra weight due to having more warriors on board, the Greek ships were catching up on the Atlantean fleet. Their initial outlay of 30 ships had been depleted beyond what Gurain could count, some ships caught and invaded, some sunk by the large boulders being slung from the masts of the Greek warships.
It was supposed to be glorious.
 Even if Gurain survived this fight, what would he tell his family. That he had been part of the fleet which had been bested by the Greeks in battle, and which then proceeded to turn and flee, desperate to avoid their demise, no matter how dishonorable their actions. They would now be the shame of their Empire, despised and ridiculed. Assuming the Greeks did not follow them and take their lands as well. Would his wife and child, mother and father, sisters and nieces and nephews be taken? Brought back to Greece for slavery? Beaten? Humiliated?

As Gurain looked anxiously back at the ships which were gradually catching them up, these thoughts would not leave his mind.
It wasn't supposed to be like this.

7

It had been many moons since Jhaerin had last visited a market-place, long before his coronation even. One look at the scene before him told him the childhood memories he had etched in his brain would not be revisited today. There were no children running afoot, carefree and innocent to the troubles of the world. There were no entertainers, no jugglers or fire eaters trying to tempt shoppers for a few coins to see some majestic feat to tell their village neighbors about. And there was certainly no joy to behold, no atmosphere buzzing with opportunity and goodwill, of carefree buyers and traders eager to purchase the latest fresh foods and newly sown clothing, trading stories of some adventure they had seen of or heard about.

That scene had been replaced by a remarkably different one. One where despair and desperation were clear, where fear and caution had overtaken joy and optimism, where the market audiences were clearly eager just to buy their food without harassment and go home to their loved ones, knowing they were safe, or as safe as they could be, for at least one more day. The markets Jhaerin had known no longer existed; they had gradually been transformed into a hell on earth in front of him today whilst he had turned a blind eye and neglected those whom he had been sworn to serve. Now, years too late, he finally had his sight back, but he could barely bring himself to look.

Even the smells were different. The strongest memories Jhaerin had of the market were always filled with smoke infused scents of luxury. Roasted or barbecued beef, chicken and mutton, enhanced with the exhilarating fragrances of mint, Basil and parsley, to name but a few. The aroma of cooked apples for the children was always heavy in the air. Since then Jhaerin had had a thousand feasts, cooked by some of the best chefs the Empire, perhaps the world had to offer. Even so, the smells of those trips to the market had always stuck with him, with an attachment he had not realized until now.

This day, however, none of those smells were present. The sweet, thrilling aromas had been replaced with the stale and dank smell of meat well past expired, fruits rotten past edible and wines fragmented into what would be better described as vinegar, bitter and toxic.

Once, a few years past, one of the Empire's Agriculture Advisors had warned Jhaerin that the food being produced was not sufficient to feed the people. This would be made worse considering the huge numbers emigrating into the Empire from all over the world in search of a better life they had heard tales about. The only way to ensure sufficient supplies, this advisor had assured Jhaerin, was to lessen the copious amounts of food going to the palace, half of which was being wasted in excess as a result of a non-stop orgy of feasts and banquets. Jhaerin had never even considered before that day the thought that people may be going hungry, that there may not be enough food to feed his people within the Empire. He had grown in a time when food was bountiful, without the possibility of there not being enough to go around.

"To hell with that idea, we're not going without so those lazy scroungers out there can eat off the back of our hard work. They can have what we don't eat, and be grateful for it!" Purias had replied, whilst rubbing grease from a half-eaten chicken leg off his fingers on a nearby servant's tunic. It had been an early morning session, and Jhaerin had been hung over from a particularly bawdy feast the previous evening. He had left the decision in the hands of his equally hung over High Priest, who although occasionally vulgar, Jhaerin had always had the utmost trust in. Looking upon the foods on offer now, Jhaerin realized how big a fool he had been.

The stale and rank odor he could smell in the market air was his doing; the undernourished and skinny men, women and children which made up the customers were made so because of his actions, or lack of action. There had been a time when this would have been the last of his concerns, now the guilt stuck in his mind as through attached as a leach, continuously pumping his head full of regrets until it was overflowing, ready to explode with toxicity. He was reminded how badly he had failed his people and how poor a successor he had been in comparison to his exalted ancestors, none of whom would have contemplated allowing the horrors he saw in front of him today to even begin to happen.

Jhaerin had been told by his tutors from a young age that a strong Emperor made a strong Empire, so what did the current state of Atlantis make him? *Weak and feeble. Selfish and Gluttonous. A failure. Not worthy of being mentioned in the same breath as my father, nor any of the great men that came before him. The scholars who write the history books of Atlantis would be better off leaving my name out of them, that is assuming there's an Empire left to write about.* Every time Jhaerin thought of *that dream* he began to get nauseous. The stench of decaying fish didn't help.

"Hey, cripple, what are you doing there? If I didn't know better, I'd say you're getting ready to steal something. You want your other hand gone as well? Or shall I just get it over with and stick your head in the noose?" The harshness of the man's words, and the realization they were directed at him, startled Jhaerin. His aim had been to keep a low profile, preach to his people from a humble position and convince those he could of the way to salvation, the way to save them all from the watery damnation he had seen. Confrontation was something entirely new to Jhaerin; he had always held the position of authority, with those around him too eager for his blessing to risk offending him.

The pale-faced youth with the Serpent tattoos on his forearms smirked at Jhaerin before walking away. The same look he had seen his Palace Protectors give a thousand times before to some unsuspecting citizen before inevitably punishing them for something Jhaerin had not even paid attention to. Jhaerin had never stopped them, never seen a reason to pay two minds to the cause or reason. But now, looking at this young Serintinal clearly intoxicated with the power he held, all he wished for was the power to tell him who he really was, and have the man seized, his bowels cut out, and his head stuck upon the nearest spike. But he knew, as he had known when he committed the act, that there was no coming back from abdication. In the eyes of Atlantis he had forsaken his people, and for that he was bound as a traitor. If his true identity was revealed to the people he would be an outcast, potentially at risk for persecution and perhaps even execution. *Even having my son as Emperor could not stop them.*

Jhaerin still did not, yet at least, regret the abdication. He was still confident that he had made the right choice. However, he did feel regret for the position in which he had left his son. Tinithius had always been a sweet boy, naïve even, ignorant to the ways of the world. It broke Jhaerins heart to think of his little boy being manipulated by the same advisors that had manipulated him, but he did not see what choice he had been given. The *Great Lord Toral* had given him his dream for a reason, and if he was to stop the prophecy and save his people, including his son, he had to make a sacrifice. He had made the sacrifice, and within that sacrifice he had also had to sacrifice his son, his flesh and blood. He doubted he would ever see Tinithius again, and if he did it would probably from a distance whilst he was standing in front of a magistrate answering treason charges.

With a weary sigh, Jhaerin turned back to the street, and began his now familiar call. "*All present listen; repentance is the only way.*"

8

The ritualistic chanting had an echoing quality to it, with every syllable seeming to bounce off each wall of the ancient caves with force, amplifying the sound and giving the impression of more men being in attendance than there actually were. Each man present had been specially chosen, a hand-picked consulate to Saritin, the Dark Lord. Only men who had committed acts deemed monstrous enough on this earth could call themselves one of "Saritins Acolytes," although recently recruits willing to undertake these acts had become more and more common. The mountain the caves were within was known by the common people as the "Mountain of the Sky," due to the fact it extended beyond the clouds and, in the eyes of the people, into the heavens above. The mountains actual name was Chiawanga, widely considered even by the travelers as the largest in the world and place of many a religious voyage for young men to find themselves and determine their purpose in life.

The caves themselves had a less divine presence. For such a large mountain, the caves were minuscule, leaving the men within cramped and restricted, dank and humid. The shallow light left shadows dancing in every corner, whilst the low ceiling meant the men closest to the edges had to bend their knees and strain their necks to stand, leaving them cramped and uncomfortable. Each man's shoulders were touching the man's next to them, each man's scent imposed upon the nostrils of their neighbors. Green moss covered every wall, making patterns upon the aged grey rock, with the only light coming from several torches elevated at the far end of the cave and above the tiny hole which counted as both the entrance and exit. It was a test of a man's' bravery and steel enough just to climb through the hole.

For every three men who were able to climb through the narrow passageway, there was one claustrophobic recruit panicking when the roof scraped their back whilst the floor caressed their stomach. Crawling back the way they came sobbing, desperate to escape back to an open environment, insistent that the heavy rock was closing in on them, about to leave them trapped for eternity within the mountain. These men who had committed acts worthy of Saritin to gain acceptance then thought they would be able simply to walk away, to pretend they had never come and go about their everyday lives as though nothing had happened. They were led to believe this, and continued to believe it, right up until the moment they were shoved from the edge of the cliff. Upon their descent from 300 feet, whilst trying to navigate their way through a turn in the cliff known by the brotherhood as "The unworthies descent." The men's splattered bodies could be seen from above once they were thrown, although it never took long for the wolves below to sniff out the scent and descend upon the corpses, gnawing every piece of flesh and marrow from the splattered remains.

The chanting ended, and each man proceeded to kneel down onto both knees. They took the heavy goblet laid in front of each of them, filled with the dark, intoxicating liquid and, one by one, from the head of the circle all the way around, drank the putrid alcohol in one gulp. "May Saritin guide us to the darkness, and deliver us from weakness, so that one day we may dine in his chamber of supremacy" each man repeated upon emptying their goblets.

"My brothers, we are here today to discuss the problems we are facing. I know you are all aware of them. We are facing persecution and execution. The people fear us, and the rulers are threatened by us. They think we are strangers, who only act in the night and then hide when the sun comes out. They don't realize that we are right underneath their noses; we are their brothers, their sons, their fathers, their husbands, their politicians and their protectors. We are the Shadows in the Dark, and for this they want to see us dead and in chains." The man speaking looked around at each man in present, to assess their reactions to his words. Most men looked unfazed, a select few nervous.

"We have received word that a new law is to be put in place, banishing our right to existence. A witch hunt is to take place, where they will try to seek our identities. They are desperate to know who we are. Should they discover who you are, who any of you truly are, there will be no merciful death, regardless of what your position outside of this organization may be. They'll rip each limb from your body and feed them to the dogs, like the naive animals they are. We must act first! I've brought you here today because there is now but one way to ensure our survival."

The man talking had always had a way with words, a leadership quality which allowed him to reach the souls of men and bend them to his will. During his youth he had used this ability for what had been considered good, before he had realized how foolish he had been. Man was not made to serve each other; man was designed to serve himself. Lutander surveyed the room, reading each man's emotions. He was satisfied that his words had reached them all, and were having a strong effect in one way or the other. Fear or anger, motivated by fear or anger as a motivator, either way these men were willing to do whatever was required for the cause.

"I was lost to all thoughts, blind to our solution. I am ashamed to say that, for a while, I lost my perspective. As Saritins messenger on earth, I should never have doubted his ability, or his cunning. Now I see what we need to do." Lutander had a discernible glean in his eye when he spoke of the cause, which emanated power and confidence to the men present. He was undoubtedly a leader of men, oozing raw charisma and effulgence.

"Saritin sent me a vision, whilst I slept two moons past. He has sent us a test, to ensure our true devotion to him. I saw a boy, no older than eight years on this earth. He was chained. He was completely at the mercy of the Dark Lord, our master's slave. The Dark Lord takes as the Dark Lord pleases, and this boy's blood was what was required. With the sacrifice of this one boy, this child, we can please our Lord and bring darkness upon this Empire. We can rule. With this one act, he will descend upon our mortal lands and deliver us our enemies."

"My brother, why does the sacrifice need to be a child? We have sacrificed animals; we have sacrificed men; we have sacrificed woman, but never children. Why does the Dark Lord require this? Have not we proved our devotion? To sacrifice a child, would that not be cowardly?" The man speaking was of middle age, but with a high pitch voice which squeaked like an adolescent girls. A face filled with acne, and a slender frame did not help the impression he gave that he was a child stuck in a man's body, and his words did even less to endear him to Lutander. Saritin had warned that even within the order there would be weak men, men who did not understand what true power meant, and did not understand the sacrifices required to gain the type of supremacy that was their destiny. *His destiny.* To question Lutander would be insulting in itself, but to question the message Saritin had given him in his dream was outright blasphemy, of which could not be ignored, nor forgiven.

"What is your name my brother?" Lutander asked with cool courtesy.

"Metander" came the reluctant, one-word reply. Lutanders icy tone had made the man regret his words, which was evident in the way his whole body had begun to shake and his forehead was perspiring.

"Well Metander, it is not our place to question the will of Saritin. Do you feel you know better than him? Do you feel we should ignore his message, give him less than he demands of us? My brothers, it was prophesized by Saritin himself that we would have the weak willed amongst us, those unwilling to do what was required. It appears to me that one of these serpents has revealed himself." The outspoken man had a look of shock on his face, a grimace half of anger at being insulted and half of fear as to what Lutander was suggesting.

"My brother, please forgive my tongue if it causes offense. I was merely bringing forth an argument that I am sure some of our fellow brothers agree with." Metander, now visibly paling and beginning to shake more violently than before, scanned the room in hope, close to desperation that someone else would bring forth an argument, jump to his rescue, be willing to risk angering Lutander further by remonstrating the cause. The mixture of actions, some men staring back at him unblinking, their contempt evident, some staring timidly at their feet, maybe in agreement with his words but clearly unwilling to share his fate, told him his faith in his brothers had been misguided.
"My brother, your words were foolish, and I wish I could ignore them. However, by the words of Saritin, to forgive blasphemy is to forgive you spitting in the face of our Dark Lord. This I cannot do. Men, seize him." Metanders arms were violently grabbed and pulled behind his back before the words had even sunk in, by assailants he could not see.
"My brother, this is foolish. I am of your cause. Our cause. I am willing to sacrifice all for Saritin."
"And sacrifice all you shall. My brothers, tonight, we shall feast on the unworthy. We shall gorge on the serpents heart, and when we are done his bones will be given to our dogs. Bound him and take him back outside, we still have business to do." A large set man retrieved several thick vines collected earlier from the surroundings forests, which were quickly utilized to make unbreakable shackles, tied around the man's feet and hands, and a thick material made from intertwined leaves sufficed as a gag. Metander was dragged to the exit, where he was placed inside and forced to wiggle upwards to depart the cave.
"My brothers, I trust you all realize I did not want to do that, but I had no choice. I am not Saritin, simply his

envoy on earth, to do as he commands. And when Saritin demands a child, a child he must be given. But not just any child, not one weak of heart and meagre to will. Not one of the numerous orphans who would not be missed. My brothers, I have been to the markets and seen the boy of my vision, in human flesh. His name is Zanati, a boy of Baerithus. Our Dark Lord came to me, and he made me aware of the importance of this boy. He is to be the greatest warrior this Empire has seen, to fight on the side of their *Fake God Toral,* a shining star in their war against our existence. My brothers, this child's light shall be extinguished before he can begin to become the man he is destined to be." Lutander let the power of his words and the importance of the message resonate with the men present.

"Plans are already in place. When we meet next, one moon from now, he will be in our possession, and following shortly, so will this world. For now, you must place your trust in me and your fellow brothers. Now stand my brothers, let us go feast on the unworthy, a mere starter sacrifice to the Dark Lord before we provide him his main course."

As each man stood to leave, one man stayed kneeling in place, frozen to the spot, confused and scared. Instinctively stroking the large scar which zigzagged across his face, the man prayed to his new found Dark Lord he had misheard the Head Acolytes words.

9

"All rise for the honorable King Tinithius, fourth of his name and rightful ruler of the Empire of Atlantis, this earth's one true paradise. May his rule be long and may his reign be filled with nothing but honor and integrity."
Purias had a loud, booming voice, and today he had to use those qualities to their fullest to be heard in the midst of the Palaces over-crowded throne room as he recited the customary words. The coronation of Emperors was not an everyday occurrence, and the crowning of the new Emperor had been met with interest by all those of power throughout the Empire, from the merchants and traders right through to the politicians and magistrates. Everyone of note was in attendance, half to say they had been to an Emperors coronation and half to win favor with the new Ruler, currency to be spent in gaining future favors as and when required. Purias was glad so many had attended, he even had several of his men making notes of those present who may be of worth to him in the future. However, the influx of bodies had

overheated the ancient room, leaving Purias uncomfortably moist, with sweat causing his robes to cling to his plump body. He would be glad when these formalities were over, and he could get some wine down his throat.

The men and women in attendance rose from their one knee salute to the new Emperor and began to applaud, enthusiastically banging their hands together to create an eclectic thrum throughout the wide, deep laying room. The men were clad in their best robes, the women their most eye-catching dresses and garments. As Purias looked over the crowd in attendance, he saw a rainbow of colours, contrasting noticeably with the dull and formal grey walls of the palace room. Blues, yellows, oranges, purples, greens, pinks, the only colour that would not be worn to an event such as this was black. The bright colours worn were a statement from the attendees that this coronation was a celebration of Emperor Tinithius's reign to be, not a morning of the mysteriously lost Jhaerin.

The Empire was still not fully aware of what had happened to Emperor Jhaerin, although not through lack of enquiries. The official story to come from the Palace had been that the old Emperor had absconded, eloped to one of the spice lands to the East for retirement. The pressures of the role had caused him overwhelming stress, and he felt as he was getting older and frailer that he would no longer be able to undertake his vital duties as Emperor. If Emperor Jhaerin himself had been in attendance to present this news to the people, some may have potentially believed the story, although most would still have had more than doubts. But Jhaerin had seemingly vanished from the face of the earth, for all Purias knew the old man had stumbled off the end of the world and landed directly in Saritins chambers. No amount of investigation seemed to be able to generate a lead as to where Jhaerin had scuttled off too, although Purias had ordered the search more for diligence than actually wanting the old man to be found.

Some of the rumors that were being spread about what had really happened to the old Emperor were various and unconventional. Some people said that Jhaerin had choked to his death on his breakfast oats, and the palace was too embarrassed to reveal this story for fear of ruining his legacy for future generations. Some said that Jhaerin had fallen off his horse and died of those wounds. Some even said that Jhaerin had underpaid one of his usual whores, and as such she had decided to open his neck. All of these stories Purias found amusing, although he could not openly laugh at the inventiveness of the tales. The stories he did not find amusing were ones accusing him of having the King kidnapped and executed, with the body disposed of in the Jazippi River. One of Purias's men had overheard men talking of this in one of the local taverns, and proceeded to cut out each of the men's tongues, so such filthy lies could not be retold.

The Boy Emperor Tinithius, as the people had begun to call him, had not yet shown any signs of not being as obedient and easy to manipulate as his father had been, although Purias had never doubted this would be the case. *Like father like son.* What he was worried about was the Greek exiles that Tinithius surrounded himself with, in the same manner his father had. They had their own views on how the Emperor should rule, as though they had a clue how an Empire ran. *If they were such experts in ruling, why had they been exiled from Greece?* It worried Purias that Tinithius was receiving advice from these men when Atlantis was actively at war with the Greeks, but the Head Priest knew that he would have to bring the subject to Tinithius's attention delicately, at a time when they were not around. He was secure in his power, but even so, he did not see a reason to actively pursue a quarrel when one could be avoided, at least not until he had the new Emperors full confidence.

Purias could see Actaeon, the most senior of the Greek exiles and potentially leader, although for what Purias could tell they did not classify him as in command of any of them, approaching from across the room with a wide, hearty grin. The Greeks were all ex-slaves who had escaped their masters and managed to board boats headed for Atlantis. They had jumped at the chance to escape to the land they had heard about in tales, the world's One True Paradise, where slavery was illegal, and all men were equal. *No one told them the common people cannot afford to feed themselves anymore I bet.* It disturbed Purias that first Jhaerin, and now Tinithius, would take advice and entrust the future of their Empire to foreigners, men who had not proved their loyalty and who had not even held positions of authority within their own lands. The Greeks had seen them as not fit to hold a position above common slave, so Purias could not see why they had been considered worthy of positions of respect and authority within the Empire of Atlantis. Whatever they had done to impress Jhaerin, Purias would have to try his hardest to ensure they did not achieve with Tinithius.

Actaeon was a handsome man, with sun kissed olive skin and strong facial features. However, whenever Purias looked upon the man, or any of the Greek exiles, all he saw was the letter C, branded deep into the men's foreheads. A slaver called Cassander owned , and all his slaves had the first letter of the man's name carved onto their foreheads. *A barbaric act for a barbaric people. No wonder we're left with all their refugees.*

"Purias may I be the first to tell you that was a wonderful service you provided. Your words were kind and true. Young Emperor Tinithius truly has the best people around him; that is clear." *Some of them,* Purias thought. As always, he was trying to look at the Greeks face as they were talking, although it was hard not to stare at the large branding that began just a few centimeters above his eyes. Whoever had done the branding had done a poor job, the edges of the C were crusted and looked like they were constantly flaking.

"Thank you Actaeon," Purias replied through gritted teeth, "I'm confident that with such exalted advisors around him our young Emperor will grow to be a truly great ruler, a leader of men. With the support of the *One True Lord Toral*, he may even be amongst the best the Empire has seen. Tell me, in Greece, did you ever see a ruler crowned?" Purias knew the answer to the question but still enjoyed the man's attempts at feigning that he had been of a higher station that he had truly been.

"Why, no, as a fact this is my first. Damaskinos and Iphitus swear they saw some King or other crowned when they were young, but not myself." Purias raised his eyebrows. *Interesting. He speaks as though he does not believe their stories; could there be some distrust within the Greek camp?* "What of you Purias? Have you ever been to such a ceremony?"

"I'm glad to say this is my first as well. Emperor Jhaerin reigned for a long time, longer than the years The *Great Lord Toral* has such far granted me on this year. He was a great ruler; I will hold him in my prayers and ask The *Great Lord* that his legacy is left untarnished by recent events." Purias flashed the Greek his most sincere looking smile; he had been practicing it just that morning. He had learnt long ago that the secret to a convincing smile was in the eyes, men trusted a man's eyes more than his teeth. "So, what of our mighty warriors, have you heard news? How do they fare against your fellow countrymen?" Purias tried his hardest not to sound accusing, as though he did not trust the Greeks motives or loyalty, but a hint of malice had been left within, a subtle intimation that Purias was not the fool Actaeon may well have thought he was.

"We hear no word. 32 moons have now passed, and we hear all sorts of rumors and gossip, but we have no official news to share. I trust the men of our fair naval fleet are in your prayers as well Purias?"

"They are my first thought as my knees touch the ground, every morning as I awake and every evening before I sleep. If The *Great Lord Toral* grants my prayers, we will have a resounding victory, smashing the Greek fleet to pieces. Mayhap you would be interested in visiting your former home when we take the Greek lands? Perhaps your former slave owner is still alive. I am a religious man, but even I would not hold against you a grudge against the man who held you in chains and treated you so..unkindly." Purias enjoyed the look of hatred in the man's normally ice-cool aqua blue eyes. *That's the weakness you Greeks all share. You make your emotions too easy to read.* Purias was making a mental note of which buttons to push to achieve which reaction. He knew that one never knew when information such as that may come of use.

"Even the most pious man would not hold against myself or my brother's retribution against *that* man. All

of us were victims to his cruelty, and that has made us all wiser and stronger. It is what has made us what we are today, and was the driving force behind our determination to help our mighty Emperor Jhaerin, and now our new Emperor Tinithius, to maintain the perfect paradise on earth that is this wonderful Empire of Atlantis. Only men who know of the horrors of slavery and inequality can truly know the importance of fighting for the rights Atlanteans take for granted."
The menacing look Purias flashed Actaeon only lasted a split second, but the Greek was very aware of it. *How dare you come to my Empire and preach about the importance of our values. I should make you swim back to where you came from with your hands tied behind your back.* It took all Purias's will and mental strength to restrain himself from a verbal backlash, instead he laughed, a throaty laugh that by design could have been interpreted in several ways.
"My friend, maybe you are right. We Atlanteans know no other way. We cannot know the cruelty and destruction of slavery as you Greeks do. But I assure you, we will do all we can to ensure we never do. Many say the Empire is not in good condition that it is..as they say…not like it was when I was a boy." Purias screwed his face as he spoke those last words, his contempt for the idea unhidden. "But these people have short memories. I grew up in this Empire too; I know what we were and what we are. The difference is not as great as they would have you believe. The people out there don't know how lucky they are. They are provided food, yet they claim it is not good enough. It has to be fresh that day, or they spit it back and blame our rule. They want order, but when our good, fair Serintinals start handing out punishments to those who deserve it, they claim they have been mistreated. I am of the opinion that these

barbarians, who make these wild claims, are the men who pushed our brave Emperor Jhaerin over the edge. The stress from their claims led him to act as he did. It's their fault, not his."

"If this is the case, then we must do all we can to prevent such pressures reaching the young shoulders of Tinithius, such a sweet child cannot be exposed to such harshness" Actaeon interjected.

"Yes, of course. I even here talk of conspiracies to implement some sort of election system, where they can decide who rules them. Like they have in Greece," Purias screwed his face up again, "and some of the northern countries. Like they would have a clue who should be ruling them. If we let these mad ideas prosper, the Empire truly will be in peril." *And we'll be out of a job.* "No, with a new Emperor comes new possibilities, and we must do all we can to stop such foolish thoughts and reckless actions. The people of Atlantis owe us, whether they know it or not, and we must protect Tinithius from their unrealistic demands."

Actaeon nodded his head slowly, clearly trying to take in the words and gage whether Purias truly believed them. *He's trying to determine whether I'm conniving, ignorant or mad? Am I capable of seeing the evil in the Empire and ignoring it, or am I truly blind to it. Am I a genuinely cruel and twisted man, taking pleasure from the pain and suffering of the people, or an unwitting pawn?*

Before Actaeon would be obliged to reply, the men were interrupted by a bellowing voice from across the room, calling all in attendance to the feast room. Food was ready, and not a second too soon for Purias, who could feel his stomach growling in anticipation of the feast about to be consumed. He had ensured no expense had been spared, what those lucky enough to be present were about to eat was the finest the Empire had to offer. Both men gave the other a curt nod, leaving no doubt in the others mind that the conversation was not over, before heading in separate directions, Actaeon back to his fellow countrymen and Purias straight to the feast hall, as fast as his plump legs would carry him. It was not often he was seen smiling, but his lips were definitely pursed in a manner to suggest anticipation of the feast at hand had succeeded in bringing about this rare occurrence.

10

Zanati had had a feeling someone was watching him for some time now, a few days at least. Yet every time he looked around, in the hope of perhaps catching a glimpse of his supposed stalker, he could never identify anything out of place. It was more a feeling of being on edge, an unexplained sense that something was amiss. At first he had taken extra precautions, avoiding walking too close to the wooded maze that sandwiched the paths on his journeys, and keeping his blade loosely sheathed within his belt, ready to pull on any assailants at a moment's notice. His mother had assured him he was being silly as children tended to be, and had told him that at his age he could no longer afford to act foolishly, jumping at every little bump in the distance. He was nearly old enough to call himself a man, and as such had to act like one. After a day or so, with no danger coming his way, he began to agree with his mother that he was being foolish, and began to relax, complacently determining that he was just being paranoid.
On this particular day, he had begun to feel more at ease. His walk, which had been on the balls of his

feet, light and deliberate to move quickly away, should danger present itself, had become slower, and undertaken with less urgency. His pace had quickened, and he had even gained enough confidence to hum loudly to himself as he walked, a common sound for the local people which told them Zanati was coming past.

It was a sweltering day, even by Atlantean standards, causing his tunic and trousers both to stick to his sweaty skin. To get away from the heat, he walked close to the edge of the path. The relief of the deep shade was welcome, and had been created by the overhanging branches of heavy oak trees which had sprung up along the path Zanati had taken to purchase supplies. The clouds above were beginning to turn, dark and ominous looking, but the relief rain would bring had not yet materialized. The crops in the ground were still dry and unlikely to grow, the people and animals still struggling with a lack of clean water to drink. The dark clouds were cruelly teasing all within the Empire, bringing respite within touching distance without ever providing the joy it was promising.

Zanati had been given by the labour captain until the sun reached the middle of the sky to be back with the materials; mortar and bricks to be used on some politician's new villa, and upon checking the position of the sun he began to hasten his step. His thoughts were based around what it would be like to be the politician, to have the type and amount of currency required to have a house built to your exact requirements. He had never had words with the man, but he had seen him more than once, inspecting the house as it was being built. A chubby man, overloaded with golden jewelry, smelling of sweet foreign perfumes and attended at every moment by a host of servants ready to please his every whim, he did not seem to be the type of altruistic servant to the Empire Zanati would have expected a politician to be. But then, given his new-found knowledge of the empire he lived in, he supposed he should not be surprised that the politicians were as prone to greed and self-indulgence as the rest of the Empire.

It was these thoughts which distracted Zanati. He was not vigilant as he had been previously, and did not see the two men in the black cloaks, with faces masked by Red hoods, hiding behind the trees in front of him. If he had he might have unsheathed his blade in hopes of scaring the men, or at very least turned to flee, in the fleeting hope some passerby might see him running and come to his rescue. As it was, the first he knew of their presence was when both men ascended at once, taking an arm each and lifting Zanati off the ground, to be returned to it face down forcefully. He did not even have time to utter a sound before his mouth was gagged by a rag which smelt and tasted rancid in equal measure, and forced far enough down his throat to cause a gag reflex. With nowhere to go, the Phlegm and mucus driveled back down his throat, bringing with them a metallic taste.

Before Zanati even had time to take in what had just happened, his arms had been banded behind his back, thick vines digging deep into his wrists, and he was on his knees, being dragged forward by strong hands yanking his hair and shoulders violently. He had never felt as light and as helpless as when one of his captors lifted him effortlessly by his collar off the ground with one hand and tossed him into the back of a waiting wagon, hitched to two stellar looking stallions. Both men climbed in and, with him on the floor in the middle, the men sat either side, with both pairs of booted feet planted firmly on the small of his back. With a firm crack of his whip an unseen man in the drivers carriage set the horses moving, and without any idea of why this was happening Zanati found himself being uncomfortably transported to destination unknown, shocked, confused, uncomfortable and above all else terrified.

11

The hustle and bustle of the Baerithus market was more chaotic than usual on this morning. The prospect of rain was present, and as such the locals had taken it as a sign, the drought was soon to be over and the gods were sending them salvation. There was even talk throughout the market that the soldiers sent over thirty moons past had scored a great victory over their enemies in the Grecian Isles, and that the *Great Lord Toral* was offering the Empire a bountiful harvest as reward. With what Saerphin had seen the *One True God* allow, he had gone past believing that he was capable of such kindness, but the people in and around the market were clearly naïve enough to hold such farcical notions.
With his head pounding viciously as the result of yet another hangover, Saerphin was trying his hardest to find shelter from the sweltering sun ahead, which despite the dark clouds was beating down on his exposed head relentlessly. The usual market dwellers were present, with plenty of Serintinals swaggering between stalls and taking what they pleased.

Magicians and other such acts performing with weathered hats in front of them in the desperate hope anyone had excess coin they were willing to offer in reward for their show. A child ran around underfoot, ignorant of all those around her until she relieved a smack across the face for bumping into a Serintinal. The usual collage of beggars and preachers were bleating on, with the noticeable addition of a new one-handed member preaching about God this and salvation that. Saerphin had heard all he needed to hear about the Gods for this lifetime.

    Saerphin did not need to peruse the goods the sellers were hawking, he knew there was only one trader whose goods would be of interest to him, and the location of that stand had become second nature to the veteran warrior. Sidestepping an oncoming mule hauling sacks of corn and wheat, Saerphin fixed his eyes upon the weather battered black and grey tent of Cranitus, a man he had got to know very well over the previous few months. Not only did Cranitus sell the cheapest wine in the village, but he was also the only trader willing to extend credit to Saerphin, when he did not have sufficient coin to pay for his goods. The Serintinals did not permit credit on their stalls, as they did not have any interest in keeping track of who owed what, and so far Cranitus was the only trader Saerphin knew bold or reckless enough to defy them on the matter. He was even pretty certain that Cranitus underpaid the taxes on what he earned, although the Serintinals clearly did not suspect this or the wine traders head would undoubtedly be being consumed by ravage dogs, instead of looking back at him from the edge of his stall.

    As Saerphin walked towards the familiar stall, he thought he heard a woman's voice calling his name, faintly, as though from a distance. He ignored it at

first, convinced that he had misheard, but then heard it again, louder and more concise. By the time he reluctantly turned around to answer the caller, the woman was within ten foot of him, still running in his direction. Saerphin recognized the woman instantly, as a brother does his brother's wife, but what alerted Saerphin to danger was the crazed look in her eye. "Saerphin, where have you been? It's Zanati, they've got him. They took him. I don't know where they've taken him." Panitias was panting heavily after every word; her sentences coming fast and almost illegible.
"Zanati? What do you mean Panitias? Who's got him? What's going on?" Saerphin had not seen nor heard from his brother's wife, nor his brother for that matter, for a long time. Not since shortly after his fall from grace, and so this surprise reunion had taken him aback.

"*They* took him. They grabbed him, dragged him into a cart and rode off. They tied him up like a dog. I don't know where they took him. Help me, help me please. For the love you bear your brother, for the love you bear me, for the love you bear your nephew, help me please." Panitias's controlled sobs of desperation were now turning into full blown wails, her look of anguish accentuated by eyes red raw from tears which had clearly been flowing for some time. Saerphin had never held any bad feelings towards his brother, nor his brother's wife for that matter, but something did not add up. Panitias had always had a penchant for theatrics, and the last thing Saerphin wanted was to waste a day's drinking because of some misunderstanding or over dramatics.

"Who's got him Panitias? And how do you know they've got him? Did you see them take him with your own eyes?" Saerphins voice was slow and patient, almost as though he was speaking to a child, and he

could see in Panitias's eyes his sister-in-law did not appreciate his condescension, nor the idea he was not taking the situation as seriously as he should.
"Some man, Siphorious, he saw. He was in the woods, when he heard a cry. Looked up and saw them grab him. Black cloaks with Red hoods. Found out who the boy was and sent word to me as soon as this happened. I asked him why he didn't do anything; he had a crossbow and all, but he just looked at me with these eyes big from terror. You know about Saritins Acolytes as well as anyone Saerphin. You know what they are, what they do. I don't know what they want. Help me get my boy back."
The mention of the name Saritins Acolytes was like a jolt of lightning surging through Saerphin, alerting his senses. He had spent the past eight months attempting to forget their very existence, to deny he had ever heard of their evil presence upon this earth. Now, he was learning that not only were they still active, probably still protected from the same men in the same positions of power, but they had taken his own nephew, a boy that shared the same blood as him.
"Where's my brother? Where's Passin, Panitias? Is he out looking for his son? There could be dangers."
"Passin, I don't know, I haven't seen him since this morning, before the moon came up. He said he was going to work, but I've tried the sites he works on, they said they haven't seen him. I'm scared; I'm scared they've taken him too. I've looked on every building site I know, and found no trace of him."
"Is that unusual Panitias? Where else would he be if he wasn't working?"
"No, not unusual. He goes away sometimes. He never says where he's been, but he's always happier when he returns, more relaxed and less argumentative. But

he was away only yesterday; I don't know why he'd go away again. None of this makes sense, why would they take my sweet boy Saerphin, tell me, why? He never hurt anyone in his life; the boys scared of his own shadow."

"I don't know, I truly don't. I don't know why they do anything, but I'm sure they have no reason to cause him harm. Why would they hurt a child for no reason?" Saerphin tried to downplay the truth of the Acolytes for his sister in law; he saw no reason for her to be aware of their true evil.

"He's told me for days that someone was following him, that he could sense someone's eyes on him "

Panitias had gone long past coherent; her sentences were beginning to become jumbled ramblings that Saerphin could make little to no sense of, but he knew he had a crucial decision to make. His nephew, and maybe his brother, were missing, kidnapped by people whose evil he had seen firsthand eight months ago in one of the most horrific moments of his life. He was once one of the greatest warriors in the Empire, but eight months of excessive drinking and under-nourishment went a great way towards zapping a man's strength, and Saerphin knew he would be kidding himself to believe he was anything but a shell of his former self. Yet it was clear no one else in the Empire would be doing anything to help his family, if the previous events were anything to go by, and a former great warrior with self-inflicted loss of form would still be better than most of the warriors in the Empire. At that point, Saerphin made a decision.

"Which way did the cart go? I'm going after them, and I'll bring your boy back Panitias."

12

"Pull harder!"
Gurain had heard this command constantly throughout the day, the ship's captain Cronias calling the instruction almost every minute, as though the ship's crew could have forgotten that they were trying to outrun an enemy that had them outnumbered and out weaponed.
They have weapons I've never even seen, believe me, I'm pulling as hard as I can!
Gurain knew exactly what the consequences of allowing themselves to be caught by the Greek warships would be. He had seen the evidence with his own eyes several times when ships, slower than theirs, had been caught and bombarded, and as such was rowing as hard as he possible could. However, having had an oar in his hand for longer than he could remember, there came a point where the dull ache in his shoulders became an almost unbearable rip, causing him to yelp in pain with each row. A sound that could be heard all the way up and down the ship. He felt as though if he kept rowing his arm

would tear away from his body altogether, and if that happened he might as well jump overboard and embrace his watery grave.

I'm rowing for my family, for a chance to see them one last time. The pain I'm feeling is for them, and for them I will row until my arms can row no longer.

For the most part Gurains eyes were straight as an arrow, fixed on the open sea before him, concentrating on the never ending expanse of water ahead to distract himself from the pain, praying that somewhere in the distance he would see home. See Atlantis. See some hope of salvation, some indication that he would not die at sea, miles away from his family and those he loved, without the chance of breaking last words with them.

The most frustrating part was that, with every able man manning the oars, there was no one to calculate their speed or the distance they were travelling. Gurain had not calculated the time it had taken them to reach Athens, so for all he knew Atlantis could be a moment away from sight, or it could be a full turn of the moon away. With time seeming to go at a snail's pace, Gurain really had no idea how much further they had to travel, or how much further he would have to endure the unbearable pain, and the mental torture of that was almost more painful than the physical.

Occasionally Gurain allowed himself the luxury of a quick look behind, to assess the situation and gauge their progress in getting away from their enemies' fleet. His heart sunk every single time; the Greek ships looked closer and closer, larger and larger.

It wasn't meant to be like this!

His eyes straight ahead, he gritted his teeth, dug deeper, rowed harder, all with the outside chance he would see home again.

It wasn't meant to be like this!

13

When Zanati tried to open his eyes, all he saw was darkness. When he tried to open his mouth, the gag around his mouth was so tightly bound the coarsely cut leather dug deep into his cheeks, leaving them chafed raw and painful. The only breath Zanati could draw was through his nose, but the smell of horse manure and whatever else was caked on the men's shoes was so overpowering he wished breath would leave him altogether. His legs were cramped from being twisted inwards towards his body, forcing him into an involuntary fetal position, but whenever he attempted to straighten them to ease the cramp he was kicked violently and received threats of what would happen to him if he did not stop moving.
To this point the men had not given Zanati any reason for his incarceration, nor suggested there was any potential he may be released. In a lot of ways, the mental torture of not knowing why this was happening was the most painful thing for the boy. His incarcerators had not interacted directly with him, except for the occasional kick to the ribs to quiet what

whimpering could be heard through his gag, and most of the time acted as though he was not even there. His bladder was close to bursting, but he did not dare try to communicate this to the men, and was praying it did not get to a situation where he needed to relieve himself within his draws. The stench of the men's boots was bad enough, and his legs were uncomfortable as it was without them being sticky and moist as well.

Eventually, after what had seemed like an eternity to Zanati, he heard the man in the front of the cart call halt to the horses, in a strangely familiar voice, followed by two crisp cracks of the whip for good measure.

"If you've gotta take a piss, do it now boy, you won't get another chance anytime soon." The voice was hoarse and gravelly, coming from the taller of the men. The man could clearly be identified as a brute from his voice, a fact which was extenuated when he added "and if you try and run, we'll break your little legs and hog-tie them to the back of the cart. Let's see how you like travelling the rest of the way like that."

Zanati did not doubt the seriousness of the threat. When the second man pulled him out of the cart, he carried him by the scruff of his neck over to the woods and placed him in front of the tree. He then stood alongside him as he did his business, before picking him back up and hauling him back into the cart.

"How much longer until we stop for the night?" the smaller, but still tall, of the men asked his loftier comrade. His voice was less gravelly, whinier and high pitched, yet still carried the same air of menace.

"Two turns of the sun until we stop. I know a good place just off the Cartemine Road, right next to the Jazippi. We can catch something to eat and let the horses rest for a few turns before we're on our way again."

The smaller man seemed sated with this answer, and for the remainder of the journey, which seemed an eternity to Zanati, neither man spoke again, leaving Zanati to dwell on his discomfort and his thoughts. The physical pain was considerably more bearable.

Zanati tried his best to drown his pain through thoughts of his savior, his father and uncle discovering he had been taken, riding into the sunset to save him and then slaying these men with one swift stroke of their swords. Or if he was lucky, they might make them suffer a bit first. His father had never been a violent man, nor skilled with a sword, but Zanati was still at a childlike age of innocence where he imagined his father capable of sub-human feats, immune to the dangers presented by ordinary men. His uncle on the other hand, was such a man. A man who had been Head Serintinal until not so long ago, when something had happened which Zanati had not been told of, despite asking his mother numerous times. All of a sudden his uncle was no longer considered a hero or even great man, resigned to spending his days drinking and selling his sword for coin. His parents had tried shielding him from the bitter truth of the matter, but Zanati was not blind to the reality.

Zanati's father had tried where he could, to help his brother, but his mother had determined the man was a bad influence and a hindrance to Zanati's development as a true and proper man of Atlantis, and so had banned him from his presence. That had been so long ago it seemed a lifetime, and Zanati was now hoping and praying the love his uncle held for him had not been lost. He envisioned the once great man steadily on their tails, hunting these mysterious men like a wildcat hunts its prey, ready to strike and rip their heads off at will. For all Zanati knew his uncle and father may be anywhere around them, ready to pounce and launch an ambush. But then reality sunk in. Zanati had been alone when he had been taken, no one even knew he was gone. If someone had seen him, they would have told his mother, the boy was well enough known and liked throughout Baerithus, but who would have seen? The path to the builders merchants was not well travelled at that time of the morning, and if anyone had seen him being kidnapped, they would have intervened, surely? His parents may well think he had run off, to join a circus or become a pickpocket in the royal streets of Pariass. With this sobering thought Zanati decided to attempt sleep, although he knew it would be hard to come by. Every time he closed his eyes, his other senses kicked into overdrive, and the stench of these men was enough to drive him to insanity.

When the cart did eventually stop, Zanati was left in the back of the whilst the driver and the taller of the men grabbed fishing poles made of bark and twine and went down to the river to catch supper. When they were out of sight of the boy, the two men took off their masks. The tall man had thick bushy brown hair and deep penetrating grey eyes, the non-flinching eyes of a killer. The second man, the driver, was distinctly indistinct in appearance, except for a large zigzagging scar that went from the bottom of his neck right up to his ear on the left side of his face.

14

The dark clouds hanging above Saerphins head matched his mood perfectly as he tirelessly marched through the thick, dry marsh. It was just gone midday, when the sun was at its harshest, and Saerphin was praying the constant sun beating down would be replaced by rain from the endless supply of grey clouds looming above, somber and foreboding. The clouds were certainly suggesting that rain was on its way. A much needed aggressive, heavy rainfall to put a halt to the drought the empire was facing. and allow the farmers crops to swell for harvest. However, so far the clouds were acting similar to the local politicians, tempting the people with promises of relief without delivering the long awaited goods.
As Saerphin reached the end of the marsh, he pulled himself up to the clearing by a nearby hanging tree vine. Still partially hung-over, he almost lost his grip half way up, but luckily eight months of hard drinking had only partly reduced his once considerable upper body strength. He could undoubtedly still place himself in an elite group of men when it came to pure might, so he managed to hold on and haul himself up and onto the path. He looked around the large open

space until he saw what he was looking for; a small cabin tucked snuggly in between a host of wild oak trees, only just visible from the clearing.

Upon approaching the wooden cabin, Saerphin was surprised by how decrepit and unwelcoming it was. Little wonder Panitias had told him the man who dwelt within was a hermit, anyone who entertained visitors would surely have more self-respect than to allow people to know that he lived in such a state. The weeds and moss that surrounded the cabin were overflowing and wild, loosely covering the sloppily erected wooden walls. The roof was halfway towards collapse, noticeably straining under the weight of a nearby half grown oak tree which had been displaced and was now leaning upon the building, camouflaging itself within the dark green vines which had been intertwined to make the roof.

Saerphins initial disgust at the house was soon replaced by a sudden sense of realization, even this rotten old structure was more than he had. Even living as a hermit in the woods was better than living as a drunk and a sword for hire in the city, taking the coin of anyone willing to give it and never asking questions beyond how much coin they were willing to give. A man once respected and feared in equal measure, how far he had fallen.

"Dark weather for dark deeds. That's what my father always said. How dark do you think the deeds of our empire must be to create clouds so black?" Saerphin spun in shock to his right, towards the direction of the unexpected voice. The man standing next to the tree in front of him was pretty much exactly what he would have expected from a hermit. Stooped shoulders made the man look shorter than he was, and his deep, jet black eyes were in stark contrast to the paleness of his skin. An unassuming face mixed with

hair white as snow might have given him a homely appearance, if it wasn't for the numerous scars running across his brow and cheeks, and potentially more hidden behind a thick, scraggly beard. Saerphin put the man at maybe sixty years, with a heavy pot belly disguising what would once have been a strong, lean body. This was clearly a man who had known his share of battles and conflict, probably the reason why he now preferred this simple life of solitude.
"My apologies friend, I did not see you there. Were you hiding behind that tree?"
"I was. I didn't know who was coming towards my house. You never know these days; can never be too careful, can you." The hermit raised the sword he had in his right hand a fraction, to demonstrate the point.
"Well, I can assure you I mean you no harm. My name is . ."
"I know who you are. And if I thought you meant me harm, I would not have told you I was here, I would have slit your throat as you went in through the door." The look in the hermit's eyes hinted at an unspoken warning, he clearly did not fully trust Saerphin yet, but in order to start the process, he sheathed his sword and began to walk towards the house. "Come, the woods have eyes, and it won't do to have them upon us. I know why you are here Saerphin."
The two men entered the unsteady structure of the man's cabin, Saerphin hesitating just a brief second before entering, as though he feared the whole building would collapse upon his head as soon as he was inside. The one room cabin was sparsely decorated; a few chairs and a wobbly table took up the majority of the centre of the room, and a few old rugs and tapestries decorated the outer walls and two of the corners. A straw mattress was laid on the floor in the far corner, with a chamber pot alongside, and

the corner closest to him on the left was occupied by a granite stove, the only item in the whole cabin that looked worth stealing. The scent of chicken wafted from that corner, and from the still glowing embers on the pan Saerphin could tell food was cooked recently. Saerphin wondered where a hermit who did not leave the area got food from, but then as he had learnt throughout his life, there were always ways. The hermit had taken a seat and indicated to Saerphin to do the same.

Saerphin spoke first. "You spoke with my brother's wife, Panitias. She said your name was Siphorious, is that correct?" Saerphin had decided to take a subtle tact towards approaching this man, better honey than vinegar. If need be he had his hunting blade tucked in his boot, and he was confident he could get it to this man's throat before he could draw his sword again, but if that could be avoided it would be for the better. This man had no reason he knew of to want to hurt him, or not want Zanati returned, so as yet there was no reason to turn hostile.

"That is correct, but what is my name to you? If I wanted you to have it, I would have given it to you. As I said, I know who you are, and I know why you are here. You want to know about the boy." The hermit had a sour look on his face whenever he spoke, as if the words were gone off and left a foul taste in his mouth. His tone was abrupt, making Saerphin question his subtle approach and consider whether a more fruitful approach would be to take the man by the throat and choke the answers out of him.

"Sir, that boy is my nephew. My brothers son. A good boy, who one day will grow to be a great man of the empire. I hope he will do a better job than I did, but unless you help me find him, we shall never know.

Panitias tells me you saw him being taken, somewhere near here. Is that so?"

"Aye, I saw the boy being taken, happened right up that path. Men just ran up, grabbed him and dragged him into their wagon. I saw them lurking behind the trees you walked through to get here, nearly went out and asked them what their business was, but then I saw the boy walking along. Looked young, maybe just over 10. Never seen him before, but then I haven't been out of this area for near on fifteen years. Next thing I know, the men have grabbed him and chucked him into their wagon, and off they go."

"What kind of wagon? What did the men look like? What were they wearing?" Saerphin could not help himself from asking questions as soon as they rose in his head. Experience had taught him that every little detail was important, even ones he had been told, to ensure he had the whole story and that this man was telling the truth.

"The type of wagon that's dragged by horses. What other type of wagon is there? And for the men, I can't tell you what they looked like, and probably couldn't identify them. I didn't hear them speak, didn't see their faces. They looked very queer though. Two of them, must have been a third in the cart as well, about medium height they were, maybe one was a bit bigger than the other. They were wearing masks and cloaks, to hide their identities. Cowards. I was always taught if you're going to have the bravery to commit an act, any act, you should have the bravery to let the world know it was you that committed it. There's no honor in hiding behind disguises."

"The masks, you're definitely sure about the details of the masks, Red masks, black cloaks? It's essential you get that right." Saerphin could feel his heart racing; he was praying that the man had his information wrong. Let anyone but Saritins Acolytes be responsible.

"Red masks, and black cloaks. Yes, definitely, without a doubt. I can still see them in my memory clear as day. Why, what's it matter what masks they wore?" The man looked nonplussed; he clearly did not understand the importance of the red masks being worn, the group the red masks represented nor gravity of the situation. Fifteen years of lack of interaction with the outside world would deprive anyone of their knowledge of society around them. It was confirmed; the boy was not just being taken for selling or extortion, he had been taken for sacrifice.

"Do you not know which people wear black cloaks and Red hoods old man? Saritins Acolytes. Evil men, who know no true god. The boys a sacrifice to their Dark Lord."

"Well, I don't know anything about sacrifices, as I said I don't leave these woods for anything. And I don't know anything about any Saritins Acolytes. All I know is they took the boy and sped off up that road, looked to be going up the Jazippi. If you want to catch your nephew, I suggest you get chasing after them. They've already got a turn of the sun on you. There is a village about half a mile from here; you can buy yourself a stallion there. You had best hurry though; the good horses tend to be gone by this time on most days. I can lend you some coin until you get back."

Saerphin looked at the man suspiciously. He did not know where the sudden generosity had come from; just a few minutes ago he had seemed more of an inconvenience and this man did not seem to want to help him at all. Now he was offering coin which, if as there was a good chance of happening, Saerphin was killed on his journey, he would never get back. However, he was not in a position to be turning coin down, so he responded "Ok, I'll lend some coin, you'll get it back with interest upon my return."

"Don't worry about the interest, just make sure you get that boy. I couldn't do anything when they took him, the least I want is to be of help in getting him back."

The hermit handed Saerphin the coins, then walked him to the door, wishing him well on his mission. When Saerphin had left the hermit walked to one corner of the room and lifted an unexceptional red and white ornate rug, exposing a large, gaping hole in the floor, leading to a chamber below. Climbing down the self-made ladder, manufactured with hard timber from fallen trees in the area, Siphorious slowly climbed down, the eyes of every aged man in the room upon him earnestly. "My brothers, our savior's quest has begun. May *The Great Lord Toral* guide him to victory, and in doing so our empire to salvation. Let us pray."

15

Panitias had never considered herself the best of mothers. She had done what was expected of her as a parent, providing shelter, food and guidance, but had kept all else to the minimum, never providing more than was required. The modern Atlantis was not a place to indulge children, as she had learnt. Those spoilt by pampering would be the first to die for talking back to a Serintinal, or starve to death when food became scarce and there was no one to provide for them.

Panitias had purposely exposed Zanati to the harsh realities of the empire in order to harden him, like one exposes concrete to the harsh environment until it becomes rock solid, unbreakable. However, despite this intentional coldness, Panitias had never had any lack of love nor affection for her child. Right now all she wanted to do was hold him, to smother him in her arms and know that he was safe, to do what she had neglected to do for so many years. She wanted to tell him that she did love him, and that he would be safe, that she could protect him. Her biggest fear was that she would never get the chance to tell him she loved him, and that thought scared her more than anything in the world. She could not face that again.

Saerphin had not let her go with him, he had insisted the journey would be too dangerous, and that she would be more hindrance than help if he had to constantly keep an eye on her as well, keep her safe from whatever dangers they may come across. Panitias understood what he meant, agreed with it even, but even so she felt that she should be doing something, instead of simply standing around feeling pity for herself. She should be out looking for the bastards who took her baby, to take away something precious from them, to make them feel the pain she was feeling, the gut-wrenching anxiety and the hollow feeling of emptiness inside her which would never be filled until she had her Zanati back.

She did not even have her husband to help or console her, however little emotional support was his forte. She still had no idea where Passin was, but she was continuously pushing the idea that he might be somehow caught up in this as well to the back of her head. It was more than she could cope with, to lose a husband as well as a child, especially without even knowing why. She had not reached that possibility being a reality yet; Passin commonly left for days on end, never telling her where he was going. She had been on the wrong end of his wrath too many times for prying as to where he went, and so now simply left him to his own devices, pretending she did not care where he went, so long as he came back to his family at the end of it. *Now would be a pretty good time to be with your family husband. Not to have deserted us when we need you.* She was torn between worry he may be hurt or in danger and contempt that he may be out gallivanting, ignorant of how he was failing in his responsibilities as a father and a husband.

As Panitias walked through the Baerithus market, she looked around at her fellow market dwellers. There were traders galore, all trying their hardest to hawk what they could, desperately trying to grab the attention of anyone walking anywhere near their stall, most weak and feeble looking from lack of regular meals. There were eagle-eyed Serintinals in every corner, large burly men with hard faces and constant scowls, cruel and unpredictable. They were keeping an eye on every coin being spent and ensuring every single drop of currency was being extracted from those in attendance, lest their supervisors determine later on that they were not collecting enough and decide to have them whipped. The chain of command, they gave the citizens grief so as not to receive grief themselves. There were the market-goers, most nervous looking, undernourished like the traders and equally weary of the Serintinals, going about their business as swiftly as possible to get back to the relative safety of their homes. Not one willing to meet a Serintinals stare, lest their act be taken for aggression.

Each man and woman here seemed to have a problem, a reason to be on edge and a reason to be fearful. But Panitias wondered if any one of them had ever gone through what she was going through, and had as much pain in their hearts as she had in hers right at this very point. The type of pain that made your heart feel as though it were about to explode. To have a child, the most precious thing in their life, snatched away from them and to be powerless to prevent it, ignorant even to why it had happened. No-one else here knew her pain, and that only made Panitias feel more alone, as though she was the only person in the market. The only person in the Empire, perhaps the only person in the world. She had prayed to *Toral* she would never feel this pain again; he had forsaken her once again.

The reality of the situation had not fully sunk in yet; Panitias head was hazy and she had the surreal feeling of not knowing whether it was real or a very bad dream. Would she wake from this nightmare at any minute, to find Zanati in his bed, safe and asleep? But in one of the painful moments of clarity which were intermittently assaulting Panitias, the situation descended a wave of grief. All of a sudden she could no longer control the tears, which forced her to sob uncontrollably right in the middle of the market square. Unaware of the confused looks she was receiving from her fellow market dwellers, Panitias forced herself to walk to a dilapidated wooden bench at the edge of one of the stalls, and sat down with her head in both hands.

"The *Great Lord Toral* knows your pain, child. He feels it. Only by giving yourself to *our lord* can you truly know peace." Panitias jolted; she had not expected to hear a voice so close, and peered up at the man standing over her.

In front of Panitias was an old man, maybe seventy years old, with wisps of light grey hair covering a sun burnt bald scalp. Average height, but starting to stoop; the man's features did not seem overtly recognizable, and Panitias was fairly sure she had never met him before in her life. Suddenly she reeled back, out of the corner of her eye she noticed the man was missing his left hand, and Panitias realized the foul odor imposed upon her nostrils was from the infected stump. A dark yellow puss releasing a foul stench which made Panitias gag.

Her anger at the man's assumptions overcame her urge to run away from this strange man as quickly as she could, Panitias snapped "Sir, with all due respect, you don't know me, and you don't know why I'm upset. You may think your *Great Lord Toral* can help my pain, but can he bring my child back? He seems to have forsaken me again, allowed monsters to come and take my child without doing anything to stop it." Panitias was ranting, her face becoming flushed and red.

The strange man grimaced. "The *Great Lord Toral* can do many things, so long as you give him your heart and soul sweet child. I was once a man some may call wicked. Gluttonous, self-absorbed, I only cared about one thing, my own happiness. I'm sure some people even went so far as to consider me evil, and wanted me dead. But now I've seen the light. Now I know the power of our *Great Lord Toral*, and now I understand that only He can guide our great Empire to salvation. If you pray with me for your son's safe return, He shall return him to you, I am sure."

Panitias stared in disbelief. *The nerve of this man.* "That is a bold promise to make, old man. You may feel your god can lead you to salvation, but my son has been taken from me, and I don't see any reason why your God, any God, would allow that to happen. Why would I entrust in him to bring me my child back?"

"My God? My child, the Great Lord Toral is not solely mine to claim. He is our God. And as our God, he feels our pain, and is just and fair when answering prayers. I have seen his power in my dreams, and know what supremacy he possesses, I can assure you. I have vowed to spend the rest of my days in His service, preaching to the great citizens of this fair Empire and lighting their path, blazing a trail to salvation whilst others drive us towards damnation and suffering, to a literal hell on earth." The man paused for breath; the exhilaration seemed too much at his age for him to cope with.

"I will pray for your child, the way I pray for all the children of Atlantis, but the power of his mothers' prayers can surely muster far greater resonance in the eyes of the *Great Toral.* It will bring you closer to achieving your purpose of reuniting you with your child." Panitias noticed that when this strange man spoke of *Toral*, his eyes took on a look of being almost possessed, as though he was overcome by some overpowering presence which controlled his mind and body, will and soul. She was not sure he was still in control of his body or mouth when in this state.

"What is your name?" The question seemed to take the man aback, as though he had never been asked the question before.

"Sanithia. Why do you ask?" The hesitant look on the man's face when replying made Panitias uneasy. She got the sense he had recently made the name up, and had to remember which name he had decided.

"I've never seen you before. I'm intrigued as to how you are so confident your God *Toral*, and he is *your* God, will bring me my child back. Until I see proof of His power, I will never refer to him as my God. Any God of mine would never allow my child to be taken, an innocent child, not whilst evil men roam this empire and inflict their will upon good men, men who pray to your God and receive no rewards for doing so."

"My child, you must understand. These are dark and dangerous times. The *Great Lord Toral* is not alone in his supremacy, although certainly his supremacy is greater than that of all others. The Dark Lord Saritin is at work, spreading his evil throughout our empire. Our world is at a crossroads, teetering on the brink of two cliffs. One direction will see us to destruction, the other to eternal paradise. The *Great Lord Toral* wants all good men of the Empire in his Kingdom of peace, but Saritin is driving men to commit unthinkable, monstrous acts, and those in a position of power to stop them are too absorbed in securing their own gains to stop them."

The saddened, regretful look in this old man's eyes told Panitias he held much sorrow, past acts still haunted him greatly, and he was now on a desperate crusade to right past wrongs in the eyes of his God. Hesitantly, he looked at Panitias, providing her with a long gaze which part unnerved and part intrigued her, as though this man was considering some great mystery. Finally, he spoke.

"My child, you say your son has been taken. That saddens me deeply, more deeply than I can express. I feel it is my duty to help, in any way I can. I am no longer....I am not a man in a position to demand assistance from authority, but I do know people, people who may help you. I believe I can discover where your child is, and who took him. I believe I can help you get your child back, but the road will be long and full of danger. Are you willing to travel that road with me child?"

Without a second to consider the old man's words, Panitias answered on sheer motherly instinct. "Yes."

16

The stallion Saerphin had chosen was large and powerful, young enough to be full of stamina but mature enough to know its limits. A dark shade of black, it had a mood to match.
The second Saerphin mounted the beast it almost shook him off, forcibly jumping on its back legs, bobbing up and down and neighing fanatically, as though its life depended upon denying Saerphin his services. Undoubtedly a lesser man would have fallen off through the sheer force of the animals attempts. Saerphin had enough experience of stallions and enough upper body strength to hold on and take control of the horse, matching aggression with authority until the horse gave in and reluctantly submitted to his will.
The man who Saerphin had brought the horse off had told him the animals name was Thunder, and whether it was because he was all black or because of his personality and attitude, Saerphin thought it was a

perfectly apt name. The man seemed relieved to be receiving coin for what he must have considered an uncontrollable horse, Saerphin wondered how long it would have been before all attempts had been given up and Thunder became dinner for the seller's family. Fresh horse meat in Atlantis could be sold at almost the same premium as healthy horses for riding.

The road Saerphin was travelling was broken and unmaintained, in complete contrast to when Saerphin had been a child travelling these very roads with his father and brother, often travelling far to bring exotic foods back for their mother. Back then, every road in the Empire was perfectly maintained, evenly tarmacked, not a pothole to be seen. *If an Empire's state of prosperity could be judged based upon its roads, Atlantis would be the perfect example of a fallen empire.* The broken roads matched the people and leaders, and Saerphin could do as little to change one as he could the other.

But what he could do, what he was determined he would do, was protect his own family. His own nephew, who had sat upon his knee from a child, who he had first taught to shoot a crossbow and the art of sword fighting. Who he had taught the Pillars of Atlantis and the importance of justice and fairness. Whose last name was still Barina, and so who could still be a man of the Empire, although clearly he would never be a Serintinal, at least not until they had been cleaned up from the inside and brought some respect back to the position. This boy was his flesh and blood, they shared the same family name and the same characteristics, even down to the flowing blonde hair, granite-like chin and sharp, unflinching blue eyes. The boy he would save, regardless of the consequences.

Riding up the Cartemine Road, parallel to the Jazippi River, would have been idyllic in any other setting.

Whenever Saerphin passed another rider he wondered whether they were enjoying a leisurely ride, unconstrained by life's stresses and turmoil's, content to wander the Empire without a care in the world. Saerphin had often thought the same when his problems had been more mundane, now he would genuinely switch problems with any one of the men or women he crossed upon his journey, let them follow the monsters whilst he worried about whatever may be on their mind that day.

The weather was still stormy, and there was definitely a chop in the wind. The rain had not begun yet, maybe a few occasional drops, and the temperature was still uncomfortably warm, close and suffocating. The ride was mundane and repetitive, but it was not boredom that was punishing Saerphin, but a sense of urgency, a nagging feeling that if he did not hurry he would be too late. Too late again.

Saerphin wanted nothing more than to push Thunder to full gallop, as he would have done on the unblemished roads of old, but these roads were just too hazardous. If Thunder stood in one pot hole mid gallop that would be a broken leg, and Saerphin did not have a clue where he would find another horse in the middle of nowhere. As much as it pained Saerphin, a steady and maintainable pace was what was required, even if it did make his thirst for a skin of wine to ease his almost unbearable anxieties and impatience that much more prominent.

A few hours into the ride, Saerphin came across a trader's stand, perched underneath the branches of a large oak tree. It looked empty upon approach, but as he pulled Thunder up to the side of the stand, Saerphin saw a pair of beady eyes looking back up at him from the darkness inside. Dismounting, Saerphin called to the man. "Good sir, what is your trade?" A trader would be the perfect man to ask whether he had seen a cart driven by strange men in red masks and black cloaks, if the man was willing to speak. The Acolytes may have threatened him into silence, and they were men who could elicit fear to the point a man's throat dried up, although Saerphin liked to consider himself an equal threat if the man was not willing to speak. All his previous notions of justice and fairness to all were being thrown to the wind on this one, all Saerphin cared about was getting his nephew back, by any means necessary. *It's not like I could get a worse reputation in this Empire.*

"I sell fruits. Strawberries, Bananas, Melons, Grapes. Freshly grown, the best in the land. What are you looking for?"

Saerphin remembered he had coin left over from the hermit; the horse had not cost as much as he had considered it would, no doubt due to its temperament. Buying goods off this man would at least allow some semblance of a relationship to be built. "I might take some strawberries. How fresh are they? Old Atlantis, or New Atlantis fresh?" Saerphin had heard that joke told a thousand times, although he had never heard anyone laugh at it. Old Atlantis fresh was more or less straight off the tree, sumptuous and juicy, full of the natural flavors which exploded in your mouth, the taste which was meant to be associated with the fruit. New Atlantis fresh was the exact opposite. New Atlantis fresh could be anything up to a few months old, and on the verge of rotting into oblivion on its own. Men would kill for Old Atlantis fresh; men often died from New Atlantis fresh.

"Old Atlantis, of course. I don't do things the New Atlantis way, never have. Why do you think I'm trading out here in the middle of nowhere? Do you

know how many people there are that come up and down this road each day, let alone how many with sufficient coin to purchase my goods."
Saerphin considered the question. "Then why trade here? Why not go to the city and get what you can? There's no shame in that; these are hard times, and you've got to do what you can to survive."
The man had not yet stood up, nor come out of the dark shadow that was the inside of his stand, so as such Saerphin had not yet seen his face. The man now stood, and to Saerphins shock displayed why he could not trade in the cities.
Upon the man's forehead the word "thief" had been branded, in large, black, unmistakable letters. The shock of seeing this ensured Saerphin did not pay attention to the rest of the man's features, but when he did, he also noticed that the man was missing both his ears, which had been cut away, leaving just large, cavernous holes. The mutilations gave the rest of the man's features a sinister look as well, although Saerphin was unsure they would have been without. Close, beady eyes complimented a small, unflinching mouth, which went in unison with the man's tiny frame, he could not have been more than five foot tall. Saerphin had seen a lot of evil in his life, and this did not rank with the mutilated body he had found that dreadful day, but even so, he had not expected to see cruelty such as this when he had approached the stand. "Who did this?"
"Who do you think? Serintinals. Cruel bastards, the lot of them. I refused to pay them undue taxes, believing in the fairness of our system. I'm an Old Atlantis man, I believe in the pillars, and until this I devoted myself to *Toral*, always confident that if I was a good man of the Empire that He would protect me. This is the protection I received. They said I was a thief, stealing

the money that was rightfully theirs. My family have run market stalls since the dawn of time, and never paid taxes as they demand. I asked them how I was stealing, but they wouldn't take that, they said I was stealing from them when I refused to pay them their undue taxes, and that I needed to be taught a lesson." The man paused, clearly holding back tears. The emotion of the subject seemed to be taking its toile.
"I'm sorry to hear that, I truly am." Saerphin offered.
The man continued. "They said I could lose my lips or my ears, and insisted they were doing me a favor by giving me a choice. Then they did this" the trader pointed to his forehead, "and banished me from the market. They told me that if they ever saw me in an Atlantean market again, they wouldn't be so generous. They actually used the words generous. So now I'm banished to the Cartemine road, serving whichever passerby's have coin, struggling every day to provide food for my child. Seven years old, and I'm all she's got. Her mother left as soon as she saw me like...like this." The man pointed to his mutilations. "She said she couldn't cope with that, didn't even want the child. She just upped and left. They took everything from me."
Saerphin did not want to ask the next question, he was unsure he wanted to know the answer, but he could not resist the urge to know. "How long ago was this?"
The man answered in a heartbeat. "15 months. I never kept track of time before it happened, but now I know exactly how long it has been since. I hope and pray that as time goes by it will become easier, but as yet that has not happened." His eyes moistened again.
The words struck Saerphin hard. Fifteen months! He would have been Head Serintinal at that time. When

this man was mutilated, punished for supposed crimes and sadistically set upon by animals, Saerphin should have been the one to stop it. He should have been the man to tame those animals, bring them to heel. Hell, they had been *his* animals. Saerphin, and the men in his command, were meant to be protecting the people of Atlantis. If this man's ordeal was the example to go by, it seemed that the people of Atlantis needed more protection from the Serintinals than anyone else.

However, for all his sorrow for the man's circumstances, Saerphin still had a job to do, and forced himself to straighten up and get back to business. *Past deeds cannot be undone, and this man's misery cannot distract me from my duty, there's too much at stake.*

"I'm very sorry for your ordeal sir. I truly am. You have suffered more than any man should. I too have been wronged, and I am on my way to make it right. My nephew, a boy of eight, has been taken. Kidnapped by evil men, for purposes not yet clear. Potentially to be sacrificed. I am on my way to find him, and bring him back. I could use your help." Saerphin gave the man his most sincere look, hoping he would take the story seriously and be of help. "Have you seen a cart of men going up this road in the past few moves of the sun? There would have been three, with maybe the boy in the back if they showed him. The men would have been wearing black cloaks with red masks; I don't think you could have missed them."

"Aye, I seen them. Seen them coming a mile away. Didn't like the look of them though, so I went into them there woods and waited until they went. The bastards stole oranges and mangos straight out of my baskets, then rode off. But I was one man against

three, and they looked mean, men not to be messed with. Black cloaks, red hoods, definitely them."
"How long ago was this." Saerphins heart was racing; he was on the right track. Until now he was just going off one man's words that this was the path the men were travelling; now he could take this as the closest to confirmation he was going to get, beyond actually seeing his Nephew in the flesh.
"Two sun movements maybe, hard to tell. Those trees block my view of the sun, so I don't really know the hours too well, just what part of the day it is. I can tell you one thing though; the men who had him were evil men, Saritins Acolytes, men who worship the Dark Lord. If you're going after them, you'd best be ready, cause they'll have your liver cut out and feed it to you raw. I've heard many tales of their kind."
Saerphin nearly blurted out he knew them better than the man knew, but decided better of it. Pretending he was just an ordinary citizen would work better than admitting who he really was, especially to this man. Also, this man seemed to have some knowledge of the Acolytes, which may be of use.
"What type of stories have you heard? I've come across the name, but don't know a lot about them."
The old Saerphin may have had a moral objection to lying to the man; the new Saerphin could not care less. He had learnt that the outcome was more important than the means, and he was willing to do far worse than lie to a market trader to get his Nephew back.
"They dabble in everything, from extortion to murder. Sacrifices are common, although from the direction they're coming from I'm assuming thr child was taken from Baerithus, that's unusual for them; they usually take their victims from closer to home. The boy must be special somehow. If they're heading east, that

means they're heading for Chiawanga, the Mountain of the Sky. Rumor has it that's where they're based, although I don't know whether that's true or not. If they're taking him up there, it's only for one thing. I suggest you get going as fast as you can, before it's too late. They've got maybe a two sun movement head start, but one man on a horse will be faster than that cart. But if you're going you'd better be ready for them, because they're not to be taken lightly. If I were you, I'd turn back the other way. One child dead is better than one dead child and one dead you."

If only it were that simple. Saerphin thanked the man for the information, purchased some oranges and whipped Thunder to turn back onto the road. Chiawanga, the tallest mountain in the Empire, maybe the world. Extending high into the sky, Saerphin had heard the tales since he was a child that the mountain stretched into heaven itself, and that those who climbed to the top could count themselves as having been in the company of the *Great Lord Toral*. Could this sacrifice be the ultimate sacrifice? Did they believe that by sacrificing Zanati in the ultimate holy place, in the presence of *Toral*, they were proving themselves worthy to Saritin, prompting him to make his presence known on earth and elevate them to a position of power unknown to man? Why else would they take a child all the way from Baerithus, unless he had a specific meaning to them.

Saerphin had a thousand thoughts pulling at him as he set off up the Cartemine Road, but only one purpose. He was going to stop this farce, stop the Saritins Acolytes like he should have done all that time ago, and save his nephew in the process. As he sped Thunder up to the maximum speed possible on the rough, dilapidated road, Saerphin made a vow to himself. No matter what it cost, Zanati would not die by the hands of these monsters upon the top of Chiawanga.

17

All his life, Tinithius had been sure of his place in the world. He was the Emperor to be, the most important man in the Empire. Now, he was not so sure. Now, instead of being the heir to the throne, he was the main man, the figurehead for the Empire, the man that all would look to for support and guidance. Tinithius had long resented his father for his failings as an Emperor, yet only now he had taken the position did he understand the weight on his shoulders that came with his new-found elevation. The pressure was all consuming, applying a constant strain on his mind and body. It was what he dreamt about, thought about at breakfast, and prayed about with the priests.
But what Tinithius knew he would not be was a replica of his father. He would not share his father's ignorance, indifference or gluttony, and he would not give the people a reason to hate him. The pressure

was immense, but whatever it took, he would be the Emperor his people needed. He would do them proud.

Lost in his thoughts, he had forgotten he had company. As he looked up, he gazed upon Avyon, who seemed content to sit in silence, embrace the warmth of the new Emperors presence without insisting upon intruding. Of all his fathers advisors, Avyon was the one true gem. A man who lived for others, lived for his work, and did not chase the material or the extravagant. Tinithius knew he needed more men like Avyon if he was to bring the Empire back to any semblance of its former glory.

"Avyon, my friend, my apologies. My mind wanders, I did not mean to neglect our conversation."

"No apologies needed, Emperor Tinithius. I must confess, my mind was wandering also. Although no doubt I have a lot less to think of than you. With all due respect, the pressures of your new found position can be suffocating to even hardened veterans of leadership and our Empires political scene, as the history books remind us no end. And, again with no offence intended, your father may be one of the best examples of that. I would be very happy to provide you any counseling you may require, to help ease you into the role. Of all the people within the Empire, I can guarantee I have the tightest lips, and nothing to gain from repeating the words you say to me."

Tinithius smiled warmly. "You do not need to reaffirm your allegiance, or your trustworthiness to me Avyon. I have lived in this Empire all my life, seen my father manipulated and distorted. I know who I cannot trust, and I know who I can. I would be very happy to have you as a close confidant, and will of course reward you richly for your services. The *Great Lord* knows, if anyone in the Empire deserves rewarding, it's you.

How you've put up with the drunks and whoremongers in this Palace for so long without giving in to the urge to slay them all, I have no idea."

"My young Emperor, everyone agrees you are wise beyond your age, and speak with an air of maturity that some men in their dying years do not possess. Perhaps myself in many regards. The most important piece of advice that I will give you is to let our *Great Lord Toral* deal with men's sins. Every man dies one day, no matter how great that man, and when he does he will be in the presence of one greater than himself. Only when a man reaches that point does he get a true gauge of how he lived his life, and only the *Great Lord* can be a true and fair judge. My role on this earth is simply to guide as many men in the right direction, the path set by *Him,* but if they choose not to heed my words then the consequences are theirs to pay. I suggest you follow the same mantra, if you hold every man accountable for every weakness, you will have no men left to run this Empire."

Avyon let the words sink in, as the man and boy say in silence for a long period contemplating the words.

"You never know, perhaps I have weaknesses of my own." Avyon winked at Tinithius, who smiled at the old man's humor.

"Well, of all the people in this Palace, I can guarantee you will be the last ending up in the dungeons." Both men chuckled.

Tinithius continued, his voice back to somber. "Do you feel my father will pay for his sins one day, in the chamber of *Toral?"* He looked at Avyon with a look of contemplation on his face. "I pray for his soul daily, yet my prayers cannot control a pre-set reality. The actions of the son may not be able to relinquish the father of his sins, yet if the seed of a man's loins can bring good into the world, bring stability and justice, can the father's sins be washed away by that act of good? The act of bringing the son into the world was a good act in itself if that son proved to do good, surely *Toral* must place some stock in that? If so, I will work to the end of my days to bring goodness back into this Empire, and pray it brings peace to my father. For all his faults, I still love him dearly, and the thought of him burning in Saritin's pits brings me nightmares."

Avyon smiled compassionately. "Wisdom beyond your years, my young Emperor. I will pray with you, and hope your father finds the peace you desire for him. "

18

For all three men, and the boy, the ride up the Cartemine Road was long and arduous, mental torture that hinged on the conflicting emotions of boredom and anxiety, repetitiveness yet fear of what lay ahead.
Every stretch of the road seemed the same as the last, every tree a repetition of the one they had passed fifty yards previous, every gull perched next to the Jazippi River a clone of a thousand already seen, even down to the same repetitive squawk. This may have been some people's idea of an idyllic ride in the countryside, but each man knew the dangers that may lay ahead, and was alert and ready for whatever may await them. However much the boy hated the journey, he knew he would probably hate the destination more, which made him flinch every time the cart seemed like it may be about to stop.
Not one of the men present was scared of the Serintinals; everyone in the Empire knew Saritins Acolytes were protected against the dangers

presented by such men. But more imminent in the men's minds was the dangers presented by the family Zanati came from, and in particular they knew the dangers presented by the boy's uncle, a man everyone in the Empire knew by name, if not by face. One man present knew the legend that was Saerphin Barina better than the rest. He ought to; he had shared the same bed as him as a child, gained nourishment from the same breast, been taught to fight by the same father. Yet the paths of Passin and his illustrious brother had been considerably different in many ways. Saerphin had always longed for the limelight, the fame and glory which came from a position within the Serintinals, the legendary status afforded. Passin has never held such ambitions, had always been content with what he had, cautious not to rock the boat and draw attention. Instead of joining the Serintinals like his older brother, he had met a woman, a beautiful woman, and started a family.

Passins' first child had been glorious, a truly beautiful child, strong and full of energy, destined for greatness. Panitias had been to see an oracle, who had foretold the child's destiny. He would be a great man of the Empire, maybe the greatest the empire had ever seen, destined to draw parallels with the *Great Lord Toral* himself and stand superior above all mortal men. The boy who was Passin's own flesh and blood was to become a legend in the Empire of Atlantis, Passin had never felt so proud.

Yet one day was all that was required to change all that. One horrific day that Passin would never forget, that had horrifically and irreversibly altered the course of events to those currently unveiling.

Passin had taken Zarias with him where ever he went, whether it was to the local market or to the see family and acquaintances in neighboring villages. His pride of the boy had been so great; he would stop and speak to strangers in the street if they showed the slightest bit of interest in the boy, eager to show them the masculine and intelligent specimen that was his child. When the boy was just five months old, Panitias belly had begun to grow, and they discovered she was carrying another child. By the time the new child was born Zarias was over a year old, and growing stronger and stronger every day. The new child was a boy, but Zanati never had Zarias's strength nor character, and it seemed clear the younger sibling would always be the weaker child, destined to walk in his older brothers shadow, similar to what was said of Passin and Saerphin. This destiny had not come true.

One day, Passin was walking back from seeing friends in the nearby village of Quarinta when he was approached by three men. They had not looked dangerous when they first approached; they were young, skinny things, mangy, grimy and underfed, probably without home. The empire had become full of such men, peasants who made their money through begging and relying on others generosities, instead of hard work and dedication like the Empire had been built upon. They claimed it was because the Empire had opened its gates to too many foreigners, looking for the perfect life in the land advertised as paradise, who were taking jobs allocated for *true* Atlanteans. Whether this was true or not Passin did not know, or before that day even consider, what he did know was that the Empire was falling apart.

Passin had walked past these mangy men without thinking twice, until one grabbed his arm. "Any spare coin for food? We're very hungry sir." Passin had never been a rich man with the luxury of excess coin to give away, and took exception to the way this man had invaded his personal space, forcing his stench

upon his nose and leaving grubby handprints over his tunic.
Passin reacted in anger, violently shaking his arm until the man's grip loosened. "I haven't got anything, now get your stinking hands off me and leave me alone."
The next thing Passin felt was a white hot pain searing across his neck, the realization that he had been slashed did not come until he saw the jagged blade in front of him, dripping crimson. A second later, as he felt a heavy object strike the top of his head, his whole world went blank.

Passin did not know how long he had been unconscious when he awoke in the bed of a nearby physician. The first thought which came to his head was the boy, he did not see him anywhere in the room, had not awoken to the familiar sound of his cries. At that moment in time he would have given anything in the world to hear those cries, the cries he had begrudged waking him so many times. He was alone in the room, and called out to discover who was there. The local physician Otander came to his calls, insisting Passin calmed down lest he loosen the stitches that had been carefully inserted into his neck.
"Otander, what happened? Where's my boy? Was he with me when I came in?" The look upon the physicians face told Passin all he needed to know, and was one he would remember until the end of his days.
"The boy wasn't with you Passin. Some people passing by saw the men who attacked you taking him. No one knows who they are, and no one knows what they did with him. I'm sorry." The physician's expression showed genuine sorrow.

"Their motive seems to have been financial; they were seen taking coin from your pockets. You've been in here for three moons now; Panitias had been by your bed but is with the child Zanati, she didn't think he should be around you in this state. You're very lucky to be alive, if you had been brought to me just a short while later you would very likely be dead."
Passin gave the doctor a look of disgust. *Lucky!* This man had the nerve to call him *lucky.* His greatest prize, the boy who would grow to be the greatest man the Empire had *ever* seen, had just become the greatest man the Empire would *never* see.
Over the coming days, as Passin fought through the pain of his injuries, he went and asked questions, against the physicians' advice. Saerphin had gone with him, equally eager to find the perpetrators and retrieve the boy, and as a prominent Serintinal held the sway and influence to ask the right questions to the right people. But even he could not find the answers they were looking for.
Some people questioned suggested the boy might have been sold, that local politicians and other such wealthy citizens often brought unwanted babies to rise as servants, children who would know no other life and work for minimal pay, their ignorance making them content and subservient. The closest Atlantis got to slavery. Others suggested that the child would have been drowned in the Jazippi, to hide the evidence of the crime, and the hardest suggestions for Passin to hear were that the child may well have been eaten, with the muggers so hungry they were unlikely to turn down any kind of food. Passin still found himself thinking about the latter more often than he would have liked, it was apparently common when babies were taken by starving thieves in the Empire.

Every lead the brothers chased up was a dead end, but Passin could not give up, even to this day had never been able to leave the ghosts of that day lie. He loved Zanati, but had never held the same unwavering degree of love he had held for Zarias, the boy who was destined for greatness. The greatest man the Empire would never know.

As the reality of what had happened sank in, Passin became more and more angry. He had always been a good man of the Empire, followed the Pillars, respected his fellow man, and followed the laws that were set. Why had this been allowed to happen? His anger started with himself, and before long he was punishing himself for not being able to save his boy. Excessive drinking, self-mutilation, starving himself for days at a time.

Marriage was considered a commitment for life in Atlantis, unlike the tales they had heard from so many other lands, but if it had not been so Passin was under no illusion that Panitias would have left him, found someone whose self-wallowing did not constantly remind her of the loss of her child. His wife's pain did not seem as pertinent to Passin as his own; her tears were lost in his own ocean of self-hate and bitterness.

As time went by, the pain never went, but the anger changed. The realization that he was not responsible settled upon Passin, and all of a sudden he understood who was truly responsible. The leaders, and people, of Atlantis. When Passin had been a child, the Empire had been the greatest the world had ever seen, the World's One True Paradise, a land where a man could be what he wanted to be and go where ever he wanted to go without consequence or danger, so long as he followed the Pillars of Atlantean society. But that land had changed, transformed into the corrupt, soiled land that lay before him today.

The leaders, in their gluttony, had allowed the Empire to become a breeding ground for monsters and criminals. Too many refugees had been allowed entrance, and with the influx of populace the food and jobs became sparse. Emperor Jhaerins solution had been to allow his Serintinals free reign to ration the food and make sure the people were kept in line, and these men once their cruelty was released in its entirety upon the Empire had become uncontrollable. They had gripped the Atlantean people by the neck and squeezed until all sense of decency and morality had left, and all that remained was an incessant determination for self-preservation regardless of the consequences.

It was no longer truly the Atlantean society; it was now an Empire of individuals living in close quarters looking for any means of advantage over their neighbors. Father not trusting son, brother not trusting sister, sister not trusting mother. The One True Paradise had become hell on earth, with every man and woman only concerned with one thing, their own survival and prosperity!

Roughly one year after his child went missing, Passin had met a man. His anger was still clear for anyone to see, and must have been a clear sign to the man that he was a potential recruit. The man had approached Passin as he was walking to his laboring job one morning, trying to shake off a hangover, rushing to avoid being late again.

"Where are you going friend?" The man's smile had seemed genuine; Passin saw no reason to avoid this man.

"To work. Why do you ask?"

"No reason. I hope you don't mind me asking, but that scar on your neck, where did it come from?"

Passin found the question strange, but the man's eyes held compassion and sincerity, they told Passin this was a man who understood his pain, who had felt similar pain himself. Even so, he had just met this man, and given his previous history of chance meetings with strangers, was not immediately keen on the idea of opening up.

"I received it a few years back. Brawl outside a tavern, you know how it goes. Young and foolish. Again, why do you ask?" Passin raised his eyebrows in suspicion. "Curious fellow aren't you!"

The man chuckled, a hearty sound that seemed to come effortlessly, a genuine reaction. "I've been called worse. But you are right Passin. I am curious. Why do you lie about your scar?" Passin stopped dead in his tracks, the strange man almost in unison, clearly anticipating such a reaction.

"How do you know my name, and how do you know I'm lying?" Passin questioned, firmly planting his feet, arms tensed, his stance defensive. He did not sense danger in the man speaking, but following these revelations certainly did not trust him.

"I know a lot about you Passin. I know the pain you feel. I genuinely do." The man laid his hand on Passin's shoulder, as if to emphasize the point. "I know you have been let down by the Empire, and if that's not an understatement then I don't know what is." The man looked Passin straight in the eye, so serenely Passin felt as though he was staring directly into his soul. "I know all about Zarias, Passin. I know those animals took him. Your son. They had no respect for the law, no respect for the Empire, and no respect for you."

The mention of Zarias brought moist tears to the brink of Passin's eyes, which he hurriedly blinked away. "Who are you? What do you want." The words were spat out aggressively, half to try and camouflage his upset with testosterone and half because Passin genuinely did not appreciate his emotions being toyed with by this stranger.

"My name is Garnacius, and I am a friend, I truly am. Come, let us walk, we have much to discuss Passin." Garnacius began casually strolling in the same direction they had been walking. Passin followed suit, his curiosity about this turn of events momentarily subsiding his anger.

Garnacius continued. "I know it's hard to believe, that I am a friend, after what you have been through. Hard to believe that you have a friend within this Empire, but you do. I am one of them, and there are many more like me. Tell me, when you say to people what you would do if you found the men who took your son, what do they reply?"

Passin looked at the man hesitantly. Before he could reply, Garnacius intersected. "I know what they say. They say trust in the *Great Lord Toral*. If you have faith in him, he will punish the wicked upon their deathbeds. Am I right? Is that what they tell you?" Passin nodded his head.

"They are fools. They know nothing about the true powers beyond our control, nor who is truly in command. Come with me!" Garnacius placed his hand on Passins hip, and directed him towards a tent some thirty feet away. Passin had not realized when they had been walking that this strange man had been subtly directing him towards it.

When they were directly outside, just before entering, Garnacius stopped Passin. "Now remember my friend, what your God preaches. Your *Great Lord*

Toral insists on forgiveness, leaving the punishments to him. Come inside." Garnacius pulled aside the fabric opening of the tent, and allowed Passin to enter before him.

Passin felt as though his heart had stopped when he entered and surveyed the scene in front of him. Tied to a torture rail in the middle of the room was a man he had seen in his dreams, and nightmares, every time he had slept since the fateful day his son he been taken from him. There was no question this was the same man. He had the same dark mangy hair, the same matted beard, the same wild eyes, and the same appearance of uncleanliness, as though you could wash him a thousand times and he would still not be clean. Even from across the room, Passin could tell he still *smelt* the same. As Passin's father would have said, this man had the aura of scum.

The only thing different this time was the smirk was no longer present. That arrogant smile that had reached from just below his eyes to the lower part of his face had been replaced by a look of terror, sheer, unadulterated terror. Passin found this look on the man's face much more satisfactory.

"Where did you find him?" Passin finally managed to croak after several moments.

"He wasn't hard to find, stupid bastards done the same thing too many times since for us not to know who he is. It's been a while, but I bet you haven't forgotten this face, have you my friend."

Passin shook his head slowly, still absorbing the scene before him. He had wanted this day to come so badly, had prayed for it, now that it had he felt overwhelmed.

"I am truly afraid to say his companions didn't survive the capture." Garnacius chuckled. "Feisty things, had balls twice the size of this ones. He pretty much rolled over and let us take him by the collar." Garnacius smirked at the man, who tried scowling back but only succeeded in reminding the men how weak and malnourished he was. He did not look like they had fed him since he was in their captivity.

Passin walked towards the captive, their eyes locked in an embrace of hatred, never leaving each other. "What did you do with my son? Is he still alive?" The man managed a full smirk this time, his eyes twinkling with evil and malice. Passin ensured this new found cockiness was short lived with a vicious slap with the back of his hand, which shook the man's head ferociously, leaving a splattering of blood from the man's mouth all over Passins tunic.

"You've got two choices, scumbag," Garnacius intersected. "Easy death, and you tell us what happened to the boy, or hard death, where you don't tell us and we chop every single piece of your body off bit by bit. I bet Passin here wants to start with your balls. We can put the gag back on, no one will hear you scream, and as you've learnt, even if they do, no one will care. These are our people, they know what you've done, and frankly they're all eager to join in your punishment. We can tell them to form a steady queue outside. Whoever's got the sharpest blade can go first."

The man broke down after that, and told Passin every gory detail. It had turned out to be his worst nightmare, the option he had not dared dream of. When the man was done confessing, Garnacius handed Passin his own knife, razor sharp and deadly. "Make it slow, and embrace every second. You'll remember these moments for the rest of your life, every time you think of Zarias."

The captive looked stunned, a mix of outrage that he had been deceived and terrified of what was about to

happen. "But wait, you said…you said…you can't!…you.." Garnacius pulled down the gag and calmly left the room before Passin started, clearly uninterested in equal measures of the man's protests and whatever revenge Passin had planned.
Half a turn of the sun later, Passin left the tent, looking exhausted yet content. Garnacius, who was awaiting his exit on a nearby bench, eyed the blood splatters up and down his tunic. "Now, tell me, would your *Great Lord Toral* have allowed you that pleasure? I think we both know the answer, don't we."
A flush of emotion overcame Passin. "I don't know how I can thank you. I've waited so long for this moment; I never thought it would come. Never in my wildest dreams did I imagine I would ever get my hands on the man who took Zarias. I'll never get my child back, but at the very least I've taken my revenge. That will bring me at least some peace for the rest of my days."
"Sometimes revenge is all we get. My brothers are happy to have helped you Passin." Garnacius gave a little bow, as if to honor Passin.
Passin grabbed Garnacius with both hands by the shoulders. "I owe you a great debt. I do not have coin, but will do anything you ask. Anything, just name it."
"I ask nothing of you Passin, nothing but an open mind. You see, my brothers and me know the truth. We know that the *Great Lord Toral* is weak. He is not the true lord, nor the true ruler. The true ruler of the Empire is the Dark Lord, Saritin. Saritin provided you with this man today, and he will provide you with much and more. The rulers of this Empire, Emperor Jhaerin, his advisors, the Serintinals, they all are as responsible for your son's death as the man in there."
Actaeon allowed the words to sink in, he could see Passins eyes becoming moist again, although he was

trying his hardest to blink away the tears. "They are responsible for the collapse of Atlantis, and their *Great Lord* allowed it to happen. Come with me tonight, to meet my brothers. As soon as I heard your story I came to see you, to determine what kind of man you are. I have watched you greatly over the previous weeks, and believe you are a chosen one, an ideal candidate to become one of Saritins Acolytes. I have told my brothers of you, and they are eager to meet you. Will you come with me?"
Passin at that moment felt obliged, this man and evidently his brothers had done so much for him. How could he say no? So he attended that night, and a few moons later again, met this man's brothers, absorbed their message, and realized that they were right. The rulers were responsible for his pain, for his sons demise, for the desecration of the once great Empire, but who were they in the long run? In the big scheme, it was *Toral* who had let him down. *Toral* who had allowed his son to be taken from him, in such a horrific manner, and *Toral* who had done nothing to bring him back.
Subliminally Passin knew these men were using his pain against him, alleviating his suffering for their own purpose, reminding him of how he had been wronged to strengthen their message, but he did not care. They were right, The *Great Lord Toral* had let him and his family down, there was only one true lord in the Empire, and that was the Dark Lord Saritin, who would before long rule all.
It did not take long for Passin to become fully converted, and he was welcomed with open arms. Membership was secret; revealing one's identity or the identity of the Acolytes was punishable by death in the most painful way imaginable, but Passin saw no reason to reveal his allegiance to anyone anyway. It

was not like anyone else had helped him when he needed them.

Panitias was beginning to see a new man, determined, resolute, strong even. She did not ask why, but enjoyed the new-found confidence and counted herself lucky the old husband whose self-wallowing and depression had reminded her daily of her lost son was gone. There was no reason to tell her why, reveal the reason for Passin's new-found buoyancy. If there was no reason to tell his wife there was definitely no reason to tell his brother, a man who being a Serintinal would without doubt have taken issue with his brother joining what was being described as a "cult," especially an outlaw one.

Passin did not know whether Saerphin would have revealed his secret, had his own brother taken prisoner, but he did not want to take that risk. For the next few years, as Saerphin elevated his status and position higher and higher within the Serintinals, he had no idea his brother was doing the same with the Saritins Acolytes. Both brothers were gaining power and influence, but their efforts were being distributed to different sides of the same battle.

Passin had never held any doubt that his brother would be elevated within the order of Serintinals, was not even surprised when that elevation was to the very top, Head Serintinal. He had however been extremely surprised when his brother had thrown it all away; chucked his career in the fire and walked off whilst the ashes charred his reputation to a crisp. The common folk told tales of the man that was once the great Saerphin, now a common drunk on the streets, a mercenary selling muscle for coin to feed his drinking addiction.

His two companions this day thought that if they should come across Saerphin, they could take him, but Passin knew they were wrong. Passin had no doubt in his mind his brother was racing up the Cartemine Road as they spoke, hell-bent on retrieving his nephew and delivering his own version of justice on those who had done his family wrong. Succeeding where he had failed, doing what he could not when Zarias was taken. Passin wondered what Saerphin's reaction would be should he find his own brother culpable, guilty of a crime so dark most men would be adamant only Saritin himself could have committed it.

The naïve people who believed in the power of the *Great Lord Toral* told stories of what happened to those who slay their own kin. Such men are punished by having the skin ripped from them and being left to roam the afterlife surrounded by luscious women, but too repulsive to even be looked at, let alone considered for seduction. Passin wondered if this was what they considered punishment for a man who slays his own child, or at least leads him to his slaying, or whether they had a much more severe punishment. All Passin knew was that he had no choice in the matter, the Dark Lord Saritin had identified Zanati to be sacrificed, and who was he to argue with such decisions, from the one who had given him the revenge he had wanted so badly?

Even with this clear rationale in mind, Passin still felt sick to his stomach every time he looked back at the wagon, heartbroken that his only living son was hog-tied like an animal in the back, frightened and alone.

The men were fed and rested, and continuing on their journey. Passin looked back, and wondered. *When will I see that familiar face coming for me?*

19

The weather had been gradually getting duller and duller, perfectly matching Panitias's mood. Dark rain clouds loomed overhead, threatening to explode, teasingly close, yet still unwilling. Rain would be a relief, absorbing some of the moisture from the air, maybe making the cloth stick to Panitias's back just a little less, reducing some of the sweat that was perpetually upon her brow. But all the physical comfort in the world would not halt the inner turmoil that was tormenting Panitias, raking around in her brain to the point her head was beginning to ache, thudding ferociously in the hot midday sun.
The sun had moved considerably since Sanithia had left, promising he would find where her son had been taken, and yet there was no sign of his return. There was something about the old man that made her feel she could trust him, an inner sense of sincerity that he radiated, but that did not make the wait any easier.
Panitias knew even if she found where her child was, and even by some miracle of *Toral*, if he provided such things, managed to get to him, there was little

chance of them being able to do anything to help. Panitias, a woman, and Sanithia, a cripple. An old one at that. They could hold the greatest weaponry the Empire had seen; shoot bolts of lightning from their eyes, have claws like lions and big dangerous tusks like the humungous animals she had heard tales of from the dark lands south, and the chance of them rescuing her child would still be approaching non-existent.

And without even possessing a sword, a knife even, we would stand less than no chance in combat against these men. Our cause of death may as well be written as suicide.

But still, as a mother, what could she do? Saerphin, brave Saerphin, had gone forward, and she had not accompanied him at his request, demand even, as she was likely to be more hindrance than help. Panitias could see the sense in that logic, although that did not make it easier to accept. However, she saw no sense in waiting by herself, lonely and helpless, every second passing wondering whether her son had just taken his last breath. If it cost her last breaths to try and save Zanati, it was a price she was more than willing to pay. She would not lose another child. *Could not* lose another child.

Eventually, just when Panitias was about to give up hope on the old man returning, she spotted his elderly face in the crowd, heading towards her.

"My child, you are still here. I am glad. I wrestled with the idea you may do something foolish, like find some other source of information and go without me." Sanithia chuckled and raised the stump where his hand used to. "Although I suppose if it comes to combat I won't be much use anyway."

Panitias was not in the mood for chuckling and jokes, impatient to discover whether the man's quest had

been fruitful. "Were these friends of yours useful? Did you find out anything?"
Sanithia paused before replying, composing himself. "Aye, I did. I'm afraid it's worse than first thought. The men who took your boy are part of an order called Saritins Acolytes. Dangerous men, men who do not follow the same laws as you and I. Men who follow the Dark Lord, and do his bidding on this earth, until the day they believe he will rise. Panitias, I know where these men will have taken your son. They will have taken him to Chiawanga, the Mountain of the Sky, many leagues away. The largest mountain man has ever known; it is said it reaches into heaven itself."
Panitias had been growing impatient, she already knew who had taken her child, but she was elated when she heard the location. She now had somewhere to go, somewhere to aim for, a physical location where her son would be. "I know where Chiawanga is. and know it's not near here, so if we want to get there anytime soon, we had best get going now."
"It is dangerous child, very dangerous, a hard ride and, should we get there, they will be ready, awaiting anyone who comes to take away their...prize."
Panitias shuddered at the way her son was described as a "prize," as though he were a piece of meat they had stolen from the market. "If you still want to go, I will go with you. I have attained two horses, mangy things, they may not take us there with much speed, but they seem sure-footed."
Panitias answered in a heartbeat, growing impatient by the delay. "What are we waiting for, where are these horses?"

"An acquaintance has them. He is just around the corner. Come, walk with me and we will retrieve them."

Sanithia could not walk at a pace that satisfied Panitias; he seemed to be cautious with each forward step he took. Panitias wondered whether that was as a result of the loss of his hand causing him balance issues, or just old age. Whichever way, she knew she could not afford to be held back by the old man's slowness; she had given these men, these monsters, enough of a head start as it was.

Saerphin, oh Saerphin, I prey to Toral you're half the warrior you used to be. May you send them all back to their dark lord, where they can dwell in his chamber for eternity.

They reached the horses, whose reigns were being held by a strong looking young man standing next to a market stall selling various expired fruits. Sanithia handed the man a coin, the man in turn nodded his appreciation to Sanithia, handed him the reigns and walked off, without saying a word.

Sanithia chuckled. "Can't even tie up your horse these days without paying someone to make sure it's not stolen." He handed Panitias the reigns of the smaller horse, a white filly with various brown spots and a mane that had not been cleaned in a long time, maybe ever. The horse stank of dried mud and was covered in bald patches, clearly diseased, but so long as it took Panitias to her child, it could smell of the manure of a thousand horses for all Panitias cared.

"Sanithia, I appreciate everything you've done so far, but I need to know, can you keep up with me? I need to get to my son as fast as possible, and I can't afford to be held back. I've given them enough of a head start. I'm sorry if these words appear harsh, considering what you've done for me, but if you ride as slow as you walk, I'm going to be better off leaving you here. There is no shame in that for you, and you already have my gratitude"

Sanithia chuckled. His constant chuckling annoyed Panitias, he was doing it far too often and he seemed to be finding the situation far more amusing than she liked.

"My child, I may walk as though I am of a hundred years, which I am not I can assure you, but get me on a horse and I am like lightning. I was at one time of the greatest riders in the Empire, in the elite. I can assure you, even at my ripe old age, and with one hand at that, I would best any man in this market at a horse race." Once again his eyes radiated honesty and sincerity, in contrast with the boastful nature of his comments, and Panitias felt she had no choice but to nod her head and mount the mangy creature she would be riding. If his actions did not match his words, it would not be difficult to leave him behind to find his own way home.

Panitias had heard of Chiawanga, but never ventured to the great mountain. Women of Atlantis rarely travelled far from home. Adventures were a luxury men were afforded. Men who thought battles and policed the streets and made the laws which governed this once great Empire got to travel it and see the sights, take in the wonders that people travelled from across the world to see. Women were expected to stay at home, bear and raise children. Panitias was in ways glad Sanithia had insisted on coming with her, she doubted she would have found the way without him.

"So" Panitias said as they reared the horses towards the market exit. "You say your friend knew of these Saritins Acolytes, told you they would be the ones to have taken my son. Who is your friend? He must be someone of importance to hold such information?" For all his apparent sincerity and genuineness, Panitias still could not shake the feeling that this stranger was hiding something from her, at the very least not being one hundred percent truthful. The last thing she wanted was to waste time with some con man, yet at this point he seemed like her only hope. She just hoped if her instinct was true and he was not being completely honest, that it was for noble reasons, which would not affect her chances of getting to Zanati. The look of concentration on his face as he considered what answer to provide confirmed her suspicion that he was not being truthful at least.

"I have many friends, some of power, some not. The friend in question I will not name, but you must trust me when I say I would trust him with my life." Sanithia gave Panitias a long, lingering look, letting his words sink in before continuing. "The *Great Lord Toral* guides our way, and he led me to the precious knowledge of where your son is being taken, or at least to a man who knew. I was sent here as a gift, Panitias, to guide you, to bring you to your son. I cannot help but feel that this quest is in some way related to a dream I had, not long ago, and if that is the case I will give anything and everything to help you in your cause. There is more riding on this than you know."

*More riding than I know? My son's life is what is riding on this! P*anitias thought but did not say. Both riders prayed the dark clouds above would finally release some rain to ease their discomfort.

20

Lutander had never been a patient man, despite his public persona. His fake public persona at least, to those who had no idea of his true identity. He had always been ambitious; when he wanted something he wanted it straight away. This lack of patience made the current wait almost unbearable, and his mood was made no better by the biting cold brought about by the strong mountain winds.
The top of Chiawanga was as high as any man had ever climbed, which brought about its reputation as the Mountain of the Sky, but the downside was that it was very windy and cold, almost unbearably this afternoon. The weather was definitely turning; the dark clouds ahead were a perfect representative of the darkness about to descend upon the Empire. Lutander wanted the boy here now, so as to do what needed to be done and reap the rewards, bring the darkness that would bring Saritin to his doorstep. Every minute that passed without the boy was a minute something could have gone wrong.

Eventually, he could stare at the distant roads no longer. He had gone through the preparations more times than he could remember, but one more time could not hurt. Tonight had to be perfect, Saritin would expect nothing less.

"Zapius, Garnacius, come here. Let's go through the plan one more time, just to be sure. " Lutander did not turn to face the men, and so did not see the two men roll their eyes, sharing a look of exasperation between themselves. They were not brave enough to share their frustrations with their leader, but they had been through the plan so many times they could undertake it in their sleep, which, if Lutander did not allow them to get some of, may have been required.

"Yes, Lutander, of course, right away." Garnacius replied. Slightly shorter than Zapius, his soft features and conservative nature often masked his more macabre side, but Lutander knew not to be fooled. Garnacius could be as devious and cruel as any man within the order, a trait which he had used many times to the Acolytes advantage.

"Start from the top, and don't miss a thing. I can't stress enough to you how important *every* little detail will be, tonight has to go flawless. We all know how much is riding on this."

"Of course, let us start." Garnacius cleared his throat. "The boy should arrive here sometime before sunset, assuming they have not run into any problems getting him here. Mainly, assuming that uncle of his doesn't put two and two together and gain a trail. Let us hope they didn't leave any witnesses when they took the boy." Lutander grimaced. The possibility Saerphin Barina would show up was a very real one, and he could not ignore that fact. Saerphin was the boy's uncle, and would do anything required to stop the past from repeating itself. They had used what

happened to Passin's son to gain the man's trust last time, now that event was working against them. Their previous opportunity had now become a threat, a threat which could bring the whole plan upon its head unless properly managed. *What's Passin ever done for us since to be worth all this effort?*
"Assuming they arrive on time, without trail, we will have the boy taken to the sacrificial pit."
"And at what time does our Lord Saritin want to see the light removed from the child?" *If you get this one wrong, you're going over the edge of this cliff.*
"When the moon reaches the centre of the sky."
"And what should be prepared before then?"
This is where it got more complicated. "Every man present must have his torch. All men know the ancient words which must be chanted to bring our Dark Lord into our presence."
"Which are? Both of you"
I could repeat them backwards by now! Garnacius thought. Both men cleared their throats, then recited the words in their deepest, most menacing sounding voice, as though Saritin himself was present at that time and would be judging their worthiness on these words.
"Dark Lord, before us we present you a gift,
Of blood and flesh, bone and humanly scent.
We present to you in the face of the fake god,
The one who claims superiority over you,
Yet was powerless to stop those,
Who act in the name of the True Lord.
A gift, one of innocence, one of purity,
We present you this sacrifice as confirmation,
The time is now to ascend upon this Empire,
And prove your dominance, your greatness.
Our Dark Lord, Saritin, if you hear these words,
And accept this gift, we bid you to Rise!"

Although tired of repeating the same plans again and again, the two men felt tingles every time they repeated those words, as though every pair of eyes in the world were upon them, and the destiny of the Empire was upon their shoulders. They did not understand how anyone could forget words of such greatness, of such resonance, but somehow it was possible.

Many of the men had been reciting day after day, yet still seemed to stumble their way through. This was common until that morning, when Lutander had asked for all men present to recite the words. The men stood in line and recited the words, some more confidently than others. One man in particular, Salinthus, a short, chubby Greek exile with a stutter, was doing a terrible job of remembering the words, or perhaps just of getting them out. Whichever way, Lutander was clearly not impressed. Most of the men present knew the look of menace in Lutander's eye as he put his arm around the man's shoulder to lead him away, as though to have a quiet word, but the man was new, clearly uninitiated in the ways of his leader on earth. He paid for that lack of knowledge dearly; his scream was piercing as Lutander grabbed him by the back of his tunic and swung him viciously over the edge of the cliff. No man bothered to look down after him, the fall was monstrous, and most were frozen stiff in terror.

"I'll be back before the sun sets. Any other man who's going to embarrass me in front of Saritin will face the same fate." And with that Lutander had stormed off, leaving the men behind shaking but relieved he had not chosen them. When he returned, every man had the chant perfected.

For now, Lutander was content. The plan was simple, and these men knew what was required. If all went as it should, the sunrise they would see this nightfall would be the last ever seen on this earth. The Dark Lord, the greatest of the Lords, the earth's one true master, would respond to their sacrifice of flesh and blood, pureness and promise; of a boy innocent of crimes yet destined for greatness. Extinguishing the light from this child, he would extinguish the light from the earth, descending darkness upon all. Saritin would know that the time was right to reveal himself, and stake his rightful claim as ruler of this earth, smiting the weak and naïve, the followers of the fake God who sought to claim dominance.

For now, Lutander waited. The time was close, and there was nothing more as yet to be done.

21

Ajinaxa Karas had the slow burning look in his eyes that told all around him to be quiet, or risk facing his fearsome wrath. Nearly every man present had been on the receiving end of his anger at some point or other during his reign as Head Serintinal, or before. They knew that the best approach involved staring at your toes and praying to *Toral* that the mammoth of a man did not decide that today was your turn to be humiliated. Small, beady pupils were centred in his wide, unblinking eyes, large even in proportion to the man's massive frame. When he stared at you, it looked like he had purely white eyes, soleless and inhuman. A sloping forehead and thick, protruding jaw enhanced Ajinaxas fearsome look, and ensured that few men were brave enough to retort in the middle of one of Ajinaxas famous dressing downs.
All for the good of the empire. Ajinaxa knew the reputation the Serintinals had received in recent years, and knew the damage certain ex-commanders had done to the post and to the fraternity as a whole. The people of Atlantis did not trust them, and for what

he had seen he did not blame them for that. But when he had taken his vows, he had meant them, and Ajinaxa vowed that he would not fail where his predecessors had. It took being hard to be fair, harshness ensured all fell in line where they should. Ajinaxas father had taught him that, before the man had been killed at sea in a pointless war against a foreign army from one of the northern lands.

His fury on this day was being leveled at a group of Serintinals he had sent to investigate a rape in the small village of Lahavina, close to Baerithius. Upon searching for the men some time after sending them on their investigation, he found them coming out of the back of a tent, several women in tow, clearly local prostitutes.

"I'm glad to see you all have been having a good time." The men knew they had been caught, and of the five Serintinals present, not one considered it a good idea to reply. Each man seemed under the same delusion that if they did not make eye contact with Ajinaxas, they would be left alone. Ajinaxa did not apply that theory, and these men would certainly receive no respite by playing dumb.

"Look me in the eye whilst I'm talking to you. All of you. NOW!" Ajinaxa roared.

Each man reluctantly raised their eyes. For all their usual bravado, the blasé attitudes to the people they were meant to protect, Ajinaxa could see not for the first time the true reality of what these men were. Cowards. Men who were taking full advantage of their positions of authority, bullying the local people who could not defend themselves, men who needed a strong commander to keep them in line.

"I sent you with clear instructions on what to do. Can anyone tell me what they were?" Silence again.

"I'm asking you a question, someone answer me before I have all your necks in a noose." The stare Ajinaxa gave the men left no room for doubt that he would carry out the threat.

Finally, one of the men plucked up the courage to respond. "Sir, you instructed us to find the culprit who apparently raped the woman who came to us earlier. We tried, but there were no witnesses, and we hit a dead end. It was very stressful, and we were on our way to inform you of our lack of success, when we came across these ladies here. Everyone must make a living Sir….and…..and we thought it might be a good way to relieve our stress."

The man was visibly shaking as he spoke. *I wonder if he genuinely thinks I'm going to fall for this, of if he just couldn't think of anything better,* Ajinaxa thought. If this was the best the Serintinals had to offer, it was clear that he had his work cut out.

"So you looked huh. Where did you look? Who did you ask? I want to talk to them myself, see if I can't make some sense out of this nonsense."

"Sir, what's the point?" The man who blurted the question was given a stunned look by each of his comrades, all of whom looked like they wanted nothing more than to sink into the ground in front of them. The man who had spoken first had gone a deep shade of red, and was noticeably cringing. Ajinaxa had also started to turn red, but thought a completely different emotion, and the enormous blue vein which stretched from his right temple all the way to his central parting had started pulsating rapidly. All the men present had seen a wild look in the man's eyes before, but at this moment he looked more like a wolf about to rip apart and devour prey.

"What's the point? Do you mind telling me what in the name of Atlantis you mean by that?" Ajinaxa stepped

close to the young Serintinal, towering over him, the man's nose coming to just under the Head Serintinals chin. "You've got a job to do, I've got a job to do, are you asking why you turned up this morning? What is your name son?"
"Tarias Sir, and I meant no disrespect. I take my position very seriously, and love nothing more than clearing the streets of this great Empire of scum." Tarias had a thick mop of dark hair, unkempt and dirty, which combined with his dark bushy eyebrows and the dirt on his face gave him the look of a village beggar. "The woman this morning, who's to say she was really raped? You know what these people are like, they're animals. Even if we find someone, it'll be her word against theirs, what are we meant to do? We're wasting our time, we should be out policing the streets, cleaning up the scum, and making sure the villagers aren't taking advantage of our generous natures."
"How you said that with a straight face I'll never know. Your generous natures huh? Yes, that's the rumor I've heard being told about the Serintinals. Generous, too kind for their own good." Ajinaxa looked at each of the men individually for effect, although to each of the men it seemed more like he was measuring them up for a coffin. "I'm going to be one hundred percent clear here gentlemen, and to you in particular." Ajinaxa grabbed Tarias with one hand by the collar and effortlessly lifted him off the floor, as though he were light as a baby. "We all know the words coming out of your mouth are worthless. When I give you a task, you follow it, word by word. Making it up was she? How do you know that? Did you even speak to her? See the look of pain in her eyes? You've had some bad Head Serintinals over the past few years,

but I can guarantee you, I will not be following in their trend."

Ajinaxa released his grip on the man, taking him by surprise so that he fell backwards onto his backside into the dust. He hesitated for a few seconds, unsure whether he should get up or stay on the ground, but the glower from Ajinaxa told him he had chosen wrong, and he quickly pulled himself up and retook his standing position, nervously brushing dust off his tunic and the back of his head.

"I AM AJINAXA KARAS! I am not Bagetius Sarial. I am not Marxillian. I am not Saerphin Barina. And I am not Jackini Arianas. These men were meant to be leading you, to be upholding the pillars of Atlantis, but they allowed the Empire to become what it is today. They allowed the Empire I love, what was once the one true paradise on earth, to become the withering mess all around you. I will not follow in their footsteps. Let me be very clear gentlemen, and I want this message passed along. The days of Serintinals extorting, plundering….this" Ajinaxa pointed to the women, who by now were on the side of the road trying to win new custom, "…it's over. I've made it my mission to bring the Empire back to prosperity, back to what it was, back to the Empire my father taught me to love. You are all men of Atlantis, you know our history, and you know what we stand for. Do you not?"

Each man nodded sheepishly.

"Do you not have voices?"

A murmuring of yes's were hesitantly released from each man's voice.

"Good. Pass the message on. If anyone doubts me, they will find out soon enough the lengths I am willing to take, and when your heads in the noose, and your dismembered arms and legs are floating up the

Jazippi and you're explaining to *Toral* how you let His Empire get in such a state, remember this conversation. I most certainly will."

With one last lingering glare of contempt, Ajinaxa turned and strode away. He was new to the role, but the men knew from his previous positions that he was not a man to be doubted, or taken lightly. He was a man who was true to his word, and a man who was clearly on the warpath, hell bent on succeeding where his predecessors had failed.

Accomplishing the impossible, Tarias thought.

22

It was nearing dark as Saerphin began to pass the village of Abalana, a trading village just off the Jazippi River famous for its Cod and Sardines. It was said the high salt levels in this part of the river were what gave the fish that extra flavor, and whether it was true or not there had been a time when citizens came from all over the Empire to purchase the famous Abalana produce. Now, however, travelling miles to sample slightly better tasting fish just seemed ridiculous to all but the wealthiest Atlanteans. The taste of the fish was the last thing on Saerphins mind, although he was still tempted to stop and purchase a skin of wine if he could find one. Something to ease the tension, make the journey a bit more bearable.
 Saerphin was using all his will not to succumb, he knew he would need to be sharp and energetic when he reached his destination. One skin of wine would lead to two, and even the great Saerphin Barina was prone to loss of balance during combat when two skins became three.

Saerphin did not see the eyes watching him intently from the trees in front as he rode up the path. All he would have seen were the eyes, the rest of the men's faces were covered with red masks.

As Saerphin directed Thunder around a right turn in the road, the men struck. An arrow came whizzing past his head, narrowly missing his neck and thwacking into a tree behind him. The ex-Head Serintinal may not have seen real action for a long time, but his instincts did not fail him. Within seconds Saerphin had rolled off Thunder, landing gently onto the balls of his feet before agilely throwing himself onto his right shoulder and rolling into a defensive position. He ran to Thunder and used him as a shield, praying the men did not retain their crossbow assault but instead chose to fight him like men. His prayers were answered, as out of the trees came three men, donning black cloaks and red masks. There was no doubting who these men were, if not by attire than by their cockiness in being willing to fight in combat instead of continuing their crossbow attack.

The odds of three on one may have been steep to some men, but Saerphin had conquered worse, and as the old feelings of adrenaline and exhilaration began to course through his veins, for the first time he realized how much he missed the excitement of conflict. At one point in his life, this had been what he lived for.

The first man was on him, wildly swinging his heavy, double-edged sword wildly at Saerphins midriff, inaccurate and ill-disciplined.

These men are not trained warriors.

A simple side step and the man was off balance, leaving the left side of his body wide open for Saerphin to open his neck with one decisive and deadly swipe of Xinias. Xinias, Saerphins sword, was slightly shorter than those traditionally used by Atlantean warriors, but Saerphin had never seen the need to have a sword longer than one's arm, precision and accuracy were more potent weapons than sheer uncontrollable power. That and making sure the blade was sharp enough to shave a cat's tail with.

The second and third men were upon Saerphin now, clearly unwilling to risk single combat after seeing the consequences handed to the first man. Two large men, Saerphins favourite type to fight.

Large, lumbering, uncoordinated and dumb. Give me that combination above small, nimble and skilled any day.

The two men tried striking at once, one aiming low towards Saerphins knees and one aiming at his neck. Managing to hop back just in time to avoid both blows, Saerphin nearly chuckled to see how close the two men's swords were to hitting each other in the swing through. He could not see their faces, but from their grunts of anger he could tell this had angered them. *Good. Large, dumb, unskilled and angry, it's just a matter of time before they leave themselves open.*

The men tried a different approach this time, circling Saerphin, one slowly stalking to his left whilst the other went to his right.

Clever!

Saerphin thought the situation was like what a mouse must feel like when being stalked by a python, the hunter patiently awaiting the perfect time to strike, unrushed, fully in control, seemingly willing to play the game for as long as it took.

What they don't realize is, I'm the python.

It was crucial he kept both men in sight, so Saerphin turned sideways to both men and remained central, with both men roughly five strides to either side of him. This dance was beginning to take longer than Saerphin would have liked. With each second passing the men were figuring out new aspects of his defensive style, and with every sideways turn he was becoming more tired, his calf's straining as he rapidly turned to ensure each man was still in eye contact. Saerphin knew one second of blindness could lead to an eternity of never opening his eyes again.

Eventually, one of the men struck. Clearly more impatient to finish Saerphin off than they had seemed, the man to his right thrust his sword in Saerphins direction, aiming for his rib cage. Saerphin utilized the lightning fast reactions he had prayed he still had to parry the blow, and in an instant threw himself to the man's left, making sure he slashed Xinias across the mans knee mid motion before leaping forward into a roll, out of the reach of the man to the left's long, heavy blade.

If that had been a shorter sword, you would have been fast enough to catch me.

The wounded mans screams were audible; Saerphin knew he had made sufficient contact to ensure the man would not be walking again, any time soon at least. The man's sword had fallen not far from him, Saerphin made sure to reach forward to grab it and throw it into the nearby trees.

This left just one man. The mask covered his face, and so his facial expression, but Saerphin knew from his body language the man was shocked, trying to comprehend how what must have seemed like an easy task had turned into such a colossal disaster. Kill one man in an ambush up the Cartemine Road, what could be so difficult.

You clearly never heard the tales of Saerphin Barina, or never paid them the attention they deserved.

At first the man's chest had been pumped out, his sword loosely at his side, a noticeable strut had been present when he strode, face on towards Saerphin. Now, the man was facing sideways, his sword rose cautiously in front of him, a noticeable shake had taken over his whole body. Saerphin looked at the man with his sharp blue eyes, patiently waiting for him to make his move.
I've got you mouse, all I need to do is wait to strike.
After a few seconds of deliberating his next move, the shaking man lost his nerve, and turned to run. Saerphin did not as a rule believe in striking men from behind. It was cowardly to kill a man without at least giving him a chance to look you in the eyes. However, at this moment he would make an exception, as he did not have time to waste chasing this man. *This coward.* With one accurate throw, Xinias was centrally lodged between the mans ribcage, one last gasp of air left the man's body before his collapse.

    Retrieving Xinias, Saerphin turned to the maimed man on the floor. A dark, crimson flow had been gushing from his knee, and as it stopped Saerphin could see the white below. There was no chance this man would be walking again, even if Saerphin did allow him to live.

"Take off your mask!" Saerphin ordered. The man stared back up at him stubbornly, defiant even in his current predicament.
Surprising, I've found one with a back bone. It won't take long to take away that will.
Saerphin placed his right sandal on the man's wound, and started to slowly apply pressure. The scream that came from the man's throat was painful even for Saerphin to hear, as were the man's nails digging into Saerphins ankle from his desperate attempts to remove his foot and so remove the pain.

But the experienced warrior knew that providing mercy was a weakness he could not afford. Not if he wanted his Nephew back.
Would these men allow Zanati mercy?
"TAKE...OFF...YOUR...MASK!"
Clearly eager to end the pain, the man complied. What lay behind the mask surprised Saerphin, as much as anything because the man was nothing out of the ordinary. He looked like any regular man, albeit a slightly large one, but certainly not the monster Saerphin had been expecting to see. *What was I expecting to see? A demon from some children's fable?*
"What's your name?" The man spat, but another application of pain brought about the inevitable result.
"Alcalius. My name's Alcalius." The man whimpered. "Kill me now. Please, just kill me now."
Saerphin looked at the man with unpitying eyes. He remembered that girl, what remained of a beautiful young woman, when he had found her, begging for the release of death. Monsters had stripped her of her life, beauty and dignity, monsters such as this, for all he knew this Alcalius could have been one of the very men who had committed that act. Mercy was the last thing this man would be served.
"Well, Alcalius, why would I do that? It seems to me you're of more use to me alive than dead, would you not agree?" Alcalius's eyes told Saerphin all he needed to know of the man's terror.
"Now I've got some questions. If you answer them truthfully, maybe I let you die. Maybe I take you to a local Physician and let you live even. At least, maybe I won't start chopping off other body parts. Does that sound like a deal." Alcalius reluctantly nodded his head, without the ability to walk or even a sword, he was truly without option. "First question, who sent you

here today? I want a name." Saerphin kept his foot perched just above the Acolytes knee, ready to apply pressure at any time should he be unsatisfied with the answers provided.

"I don't know a name." Pressure was applied to the mans knee again, and Saerphin made a chopping motion with Xinias towards the mans shoulder, as though he was about to swing and take off the mans whole arm clean off.

"Okay, okay. Lutander. The man who sent me is called Lutander." The man paused, as if to consider whether to continue, before deciding he really had no choice.

"He told us to come and ambush you on the way up the road. I said we needed more, to face the famous Saerphin Barina, but he said three people should be plenty. He said you were washed up, and that you'd probably be too drunk to even fight back."

Saerphin chuckled. *So it seems my reputation for being a drunk has surpassed my reputation as a great warrior.* "I didn't want to come, but I had no choice. When Lutander speaks, people listen. He has that power."

"The great Saerphin Barina huh. Where do you think flattery will get you? Next question. Where's the boy. And if you say what boy, I really will start lopping off body parts." Saerphin could tell by the fear in Alcalius's eyes that he had ripped all the resolve from him, he was his to milk all the information he needed.

"The boy, he's going up the Cartemine Road as we speak. Towards Chiawanga. They want him for some big sacrifice. Apparently he's special, Lutander says Saritin told him he's destined to be the greatest Atlantean that lived. That's why he's been chosen for sacrifice, to show Saritin our devotion to him." To Saerphin's displeasure the man closed his eyes and

seemed to murmur, as though making a silent prayer to his dark lord.
He can't help you here.
"Stop that. How long ago did they leave? And how many men are at Chiawanga awaiting Zanati? Give me a truthful number."
"Maybe fifty, maybe hundred. I don't know the exact figure. We're an outlaw group, we don't exactly keep a register. Couldn't have been more than a turn of the sun ago they moved past here, the sun was somewhere near the centre of the sky when they passed us. We came from Chiawanga, with our instructions from Lutander. You can still catch him if you hurry."
Alcalius had a hopeful look on his face, as though he expected his enthusiasm and assistance to cause Saerphin to forget his reason for being there today and forgive and forget. Saerphin was not in a forgiving mood, and at this point had gleaned all the useful information he needed out of the man. However, considering who this man was and what he was a part of, Saerphin could not bring himself to allow an easy death. Four clean strokes of his blade took all four of the man's limbs clean off, Saerphin called Thunder who had been grazing at a nearby patch of grass and left the man for the wolves to finish what he had started.
I must find out more of this Lutander.

23

Emperor Tinithius looked even younger than his 14 years on the planet suggested, with soft features, milky eyes and a frame so minute and feeble he appeared sickly. Wispy blonde hair, so fair it was almost white, did little more to present an appearance of maturity, Tinithius knew he was perceived as weak and to be manipulated and as much as he understood why, he did not respect it. His father had directly taught him very little, but his reign had taught him more than any words ever could. Weak men were manipulated, controlled by men of greater minds and often of dubious motives. Men of greater cunning persuaded and cajoled until they got what they wanted, and the weak and feeble allowed them, either too frightened or too indifferent to stop them from taking what they wanted.

My father was weak. Greedy. Preoccupied by the things that did not matter, too blind to see the evils happening in front of his very eyes! I am not that man! I will not leave that legacy!

Even at the tender age of fourteen, Tinithius knew he was stronger than his father, smarter even. He had seen the Empire for what it was since the age he was old enough to read, to devour books describing in intimate details the beauty of Atlantis, then look at the markets and see the contrast, the ugliness the Empire had fallen to. His father and his closest advisors had done what they could to hide Tinithius from the brutal truth of how far the Empire had fallen, but the ruse could not last forever. And now, years later, Tinithius knew exactly what state this once beautiful metropolis was in, this land which he now ruled.

His father's influence in his growth as a man had been minimal, and Tinithius had received little female guidance, his mother having died conceiving him. When he was younger, whilst his father had been out whoring or feasting, he had often prayed to *Toral* to undo his previous decision, and grant Tinithius his mother back. He wanted to at least meet her and gain some perspective of who he was, where he had come from. He did not believe he could have come from the loins of his ignorant, ever happy, whore mongering father, regardless of what he was told. He was better than that, and had been from an early age.

The days of Tinithius praying for such things were over. He was old enough to know what praying for such things got him, and knew his prayers were better served on the souls of his people, those who knew no better than what they had become. What his father had let them become.

Looking around the table at his council members, Emperor Tinithius knew the majority of the men present were as guilty as his father himself had been. Equally greedy, equally ignorant to the suffering of their fellow Atlanteans, but unlike his father they did not appear to have changed their ways, repented in any manner. The news they had just received was shocking, yet no man present, bar one or two who were clearly acting to impress their new Emperor, looked the least bit shocked or concerned. The men were talking amongst themselves, some clearly even sharing a joke at the back end of the table. Tinithius could stand no more, and with one swift motion slammed his fist violently onto the heavy wooden table, making a considerable thud for such a feeble body. The impact sent vibrations all the way down to the far end of the table, everyone present was quiet immediately.

"ENOUGH! You all sit there and talk amongst yourselves, share your jokes, pretend that all is fine in the Empire. You've pretended for so long, some of you may even believe all IS fine in the Empire." Tinithius's voice was shaking as he spoke, more in rage than nervousness, and he stopped to compose himself. His normally high, sweet voice was now laced with malice and anger, to the point it came out as an animalistic growl.

"Well, my friends, I can tell you one thing. All IS NOT OK in the Empire. My father may have been satisfied with the way things were run, but I am not. We have just heard news of a boy being taken from his mother, kidnapped by outlaws who do not abide by our laws, and you act like all is fine, as though this is an everyday occurrence."

Tinithius looked slowly around the room, from man to man, measuring up each present council member's reaction. Some looked ashamed, some shocked, some indignant. Tinithius knew it was important to remember each man's reaction, to gauge their uses to him and determine whether they had any role to play in his regime. As much as he despised the games and the politics, he knew their worth, and knew he

would need to think tactically if he were to gain the upper hand over these men, and use each man to their best purpose.
Before Tinithius could continue, Purias intercepted. "My young Emperor, I think you are taking the situation a bit too personally. So some child has been taken. What can we do about it? Frankly, it probably is an everyday thing. Now, everybody present knows, I am as pious as they come," Tinithius noticed more than a few raised eyebrows throughout the hall, "and I will be praying for this boy's safe return, or should that not occur that the *Great Lord Toral* will guide him a safe passage to his Glorious Kingdom of Paradise, but what more can we do? Would you send your men to look for this boy? The Palace is stretched enough for men as it is, with our Army off at sea fighting the Greeks. Who would protect you, my young Emperor?"
"Protect us I assume you mean? Or, more accurately, you?"
Purias looked at Tinithius with apparent genuine insult, although Tinithius had known him for long enough to know it was feigned. *This one could play the stage in the legendary Athenian Theatres.*
"I am truly offended you feel a man such as myself, with my holy position, is more concerned by his own personal welfare than that of his beloved Emperor? Or our people? I hope you do not truly believe this."
"I truly believe that you, as well as every other man present, is equally culpable in the state of the Empire as my father. And the next time you use that condescending tone with me, or call me your "Young Emperor," I'll have your head on a stick, you pompous imbecile."
A large gasp seemed to eminate from each person present, as though they had never heard an Emperor raise their voice before, or at least not with such

venom. And no man present had ever seen anyone talk to Purias in such a way, whose face had now gone bright red, more in rage than embarrassment. He started to compose a reply, remaining as calm and respectful as possible, but Tinithius cut him off.

"Purias, let me be clear, I do not trust you. Never have, and never will. You claim to be a pious man, yet all I see you do is host your fancy feasts, drink your fancy wine and indulge yourself with your fancy whores. I've seen this since I was a child, and always wondered why you were considered so important? The people of this Empire are suffering, and you do nothing to help. When is the last time you left the Palace? Went to the streets and helped those in need? If you are considered so important in the Empire, why don't you ever do anything to help those who need it?"

Every eye in the room was now on Purias, who, for what was the first time any man present could remember, was lost for words. The usually bawdy priest was taken aback by the viciousness of the sudden unrelenting attack, and could only stare back with his mouth wide open, his beady eyes darting around the room, looking for support from anyone who would provide it. He received none.

Tinithius continued. "For years I have seen you manipulating my father, feeding him information to further your cause, strengthen your position, and fatten your pocket. I may be young, but I am not blind, and I am not feeble. Men, take Purias to the dungeons. He will have his day in court, and answer to charges of neglect of duty. May the *Great Lord Toral* forgive you for your neglect of him, I certainly cannot."

If every man present had been shocked at the beginning of the verbal assault, they were now positively speechless as the Palace guards descended upon the large priest, who was so stunned he put up no fight as several guards surrounded him and placed his arms behind his back, tying them with vine. As the shock washed over, and he was lifted to his feet by several men pulling his eloquent tunic, a sense of anger came over Purias. "My Emperor, you cannot do this. Your father knew better. Tell these men to get their stinking hands off me, this tunic is made of the finest fabrics. Tell them take their hands off me lest I have them taken off when I'm found innocent. Tell them, tell them now my Emperor." Purias's voice trailed off as he was dragged by several men into the large marble hall adjacent to the Council Meeting Chamber, before being unceremoniously made to make a left turn and marshaled in the direction of the dungeons.

Tinithius waited until his cries of protest were so far in the distance they could no longer be heard. "I trust I have your attention, gentlemen." Each man present nodded, most still open mouthed and wide-eyed.

"My father has apparently seen the light, and has answered the *Great Lord Torals* call to undertake his work on this earth. A few years too late if you ask me, but that is irrelevant now. My father is and was many things, but a liar has never been one of them. When he passes a message to us, through an intermediary whom I trust more than anyone on this planet, then I can assure you all I take that message seriously. There is a child in danger, and the reason he is in danger is that we, and I will be very loose with the term we, have allowed this Empire to be corrupted to the point children can be taken without fear of consequence." Tinithius paused for effect, each man in the room hanging off his every word.

"Well that Empire's existence ends now. I want 50 of our best men to ride at once to Chiawanga, to face these Saritins Acolytes, and reclaim this child. I want as many of them left alive as possible, so they can answer to me in court, and face the consequences our laws demand. Our people must see these men paying the consequences for their actions, lest every man deems it acceptable to defy our laws with impunity."

Tinithius could see a few dubious looking faces, he was aware as anyone how undermanned the Palace was, but there came a time when a decision had to be made, when the moral ambiguity of the Empire was more important than his own personal security, or that of any of these men, and Tinithius knew he was at that crossroad. To allow this monstrosity to happen would be to open the doors and allow evil into the Empire, to climb into bed with the *Dark Lord Saritin* himself in all his wickedness and embrace him in his fight against good. Under no circumstances could that be allowed to happen.

"Go, do as your told, and don't fail me." The room quickly emptied, several men bowing before their Emperor as they exited.

As Tinithius stared out the Council Chambers tall windows, he could see the dark clouds becoming more and more threatening in the distance. *How dark the deeds of our Empire indeed.*

24

Saerphin had seen a figure in the distance, blocking the road, for some time now. At first he had considered whoever the person was to be most likely some lost traveler, or a beggar blocking passage of anyone until they provided coin or food. He had seen plenty of the kind thus far in his journey, and received little to no problems from them, largely because the second they saw Xinias they skulked away as swiftly as they could. But as he neared the figure, which was slowly becoming more than just a dark silhouette in the distance, his survival instincts started to kick in. Adrenaline started pumping rapidly around his body, increasing his heart rate, and his breathing began to quicken, as though he had run his journey thus far on foot. Whatever danger lay in his path, he was ready.
There was something about the way the figure was standing that was what made Saerphin uneasy. He had know that the Saritins Acolytes would not leave just one trap for him on this road, but he had assumed he should be looking out for an ambush, not a sole assailant offering him single combat. That this man,

he could now clearly make out from the outline that it was a man, would be brazen enough to await him in full view made him more cautious than if he could see men behind the trees with crossbows in hand. He tapered his urge to gallop full speed, as he would have done as a younger man. Saerphin had learnt, the hard way, the dangers that came when acting without analyzing the situation first.

As Saerphin grew nearer to the man, close enough to get a vague look at his figure, a realization hit him. This was no ordinary man. This man was a giant, a monster. It could only be one man, a man whose legend equaled Saerphins own throughout the Empire. Prization, *the man with no soul*.

Prization was an Atlantean by birth, but had travelled as a mercenary since before Saerphin could remember, selling his sword for coin all over the civilized world, and even into the uncivilized. Saerphin had heard tales of his prowess in battle from almost every land he had ever heard of. Greece, the dark lands below, the spice lands to the east, the savage lands north, even as far as the white lands way north, farther than most men of the Empire had ever dreamed of travelling. Prization had been there, and he had bested the best. He was renowned throughout every land worth knowing, and today he was calmly standing in the middle of the road in front of the ex-Head Serintinal, hand on sword, clear purpose in mind.

Saerphin had heard rumors of Prizations size; he had never actually seen the man in the flesh, but even those accusations which had seemed exaggerated at the time of hearing them seemed to be short-selling the man now that Saerphin could see him with his own eyes. A healthy three heads taller than Saerphin, Prization had the thick, muscle ridden arms of a man who had worked manually as a child, and a chest which matched any ale barrel Saerphin had ever seen in the local taverns. Dark olive skin, a pronounced nose and light brown eyes suggested some Greek origins, although by the size of the man Saerphin would have to consider only The Great Lord Toral himself could have molded such a perfect warrior, or the Dark Lord Saritin. Saerphin had heard tales of the man's temper and sadistic ways, when his name was mentioned in gossip and tales it was often said he had no soul, due to the wicked deeds he was rumored to have done, and coupled with his current paymasters he was more prone to believe the latter to be his creator.

However perfect a warrior you may be, however vicious and brutal a man you may be, I cannot allow you to stand in my way. There is too much at stake.

As he neared the mammoth of a man, Saerphin steeled himself, allowing the righteousness of his purpose to send strength and calm coursing through his veins. *The Great Lord Toral is on my side, and with his power, no man in this Empire can stand in my way!*

Saerphin was now in hearing distance of the man, close enough to examine the numerous scars running across his body. *You may feel they make you look tough, I know they make you look mortal. Vulnerable. Killable.*

"I do not want to hurt you, Prization. I know who you are, and you may know who I am. Or you may not. Whichever way, I do not truly believe you want us to come to conflict today. I am a man on a mission, with the strength and guidance of *The Great Lord Toral* on my side, I will not be stopped by any man." Saerphin noticed the sides of the big man's mouth raise slightly, an arrogant smirk. *This man believes this battle is already won, and thinks I am solely a coward trying to avoid conflict.*

"Your current pay masters are not all they may have told you they are. They are evil men, monsters, way worse than yourself. Have they told you why I am going after them? The purpose of my mission?"

Prization took a second to consider the question, before venomously spitting a large lump of phlegm onto the ground between the two men, falling just a foot or two short of the horse's hooves. "I could not care less for their reasons. I don't have to listen to whatever reasons people tell me. People lie when they give reasons, all people. I take coin, I kill who I'm told. I don't ask, they don't tell, I don't care." The smirk was ever present on Prizations face as he spoke, he was enjoying this.

"Now, I have heard tales of you...*Saerphin*," the words were laced with contempt, "and I know people think you are a great warrior. Why don't you pull out that sword and let a truly great warrior show you how to fight? Not that you'll ever get the chance to put into practice what you learn here today."

The big man's arrogance angered Saerphin, but did not surprise him. A man did not become a legend throughout several lands such as Prization had without a level of self-belief bordering on believing one's self invinciblity, and Saerphin could tell this man could not contemplate being beaten today, or any day for that matter.

Oh Great Lord Toral, grant me strength to smite this wicked foe!

Not usually a pious man by any stretch, even less so in recent years, Saerphin knew he would need all the help he could get.

Shrugging nonchalantly to attempt to convey some sort of control, a careless ease which might make this monstrous warrior think twice about whether this battle was won already, Saerphin replied "As you say big man. But don't let it be said I didn't give you a way out, not that you'll be saying anything after today anyway."

The smirk on Prizations face angered Saerphin further, as he climbed down from Thunder and both men unsheathed their swords. This would be the second time within the last few turns of the sun that Xinias would taste combat, Saerphin prayed his trusty steel would stay hungry once more and feed off this mercenary's flesh.

Both men were now within yards of each other, knees slightly bent, sword in front, positioned to block any sudden attacks. Both men were circling around, looking for weaknesses in the other man's defence to exploit. Prization favored a long sword, heavy and solid, so sharp Saerphin could see the sun shine off its edges. If one swing caught him he knew it would be all over. Any other opponent and he would be confident the sword was too large for them to control, but he did not need to take a second look at Prization's arms to know not to pin his hopes on such thoughts in this battle. Prization looked like he could swing a horse with full control if he so desired.

Prization, growing impatient with the constant circling, was the first to strike. A well controlled right arm cut from left to right almost caught Saerphin across his throat, but the experienced warrior managed to hop backwards in time to avoid the contact. He attempted a stabbing motion at the big man's chest which was powerfully parried away, the familiar clang of steel on steel strangely relieving to Saerphin. The politics, the games, the chasing he could not cope with, steel on steel was his way of dealing with issues, man on man, fighting with honor and integrity.

The circling returned, Saerphin noticing the big man was out of breath from the first furor. *Most opponents you can catch with that first swipe, not many come back at you for a second.* Saerphin knew it was time to press his advantage as Prization was struggling to catch his breath, and quickened his stalking, waiting for an opportunity to strike like a cobra stalking a mouse, ready to pounce the second he was his opportunity.

The chance came, but Saerphin was too slow. He raised his sword to swing a second too late, and Prization had already raised his sword to block, anticipating the move. Prization feigned the assault then retreated half a foot back to safety. The circling continued.

As both men continued to swirl in a circle of destiny, a game where there could only be one winner and the loser lost all, they began to, without noticing, move gradually away from the centre of the road, towards the fast flowing Jazippi River, whose steep banks were now just a few feet from the two men.

Saerphin was the first to notice, as his right foot caught on a shrub on the river bank. He began to stumble, and in doing so took his eyes off his big opponent. That split second was all it took for Prization to pounce. With a massive roar, his powerful long sword was hauled right to left, across Saerphins midriff, cutting deep into meaty flesh, cracking ribs. The impact of the heavy blow sent Saerphin sprawling backwards, straight into the river's unyielding path. As the man with no soul watched without a flinch of emotion, Saerphin was dragged under the water in the heavy current, before even a whimper could leave his throat.

Prization spat into the river after him before walking back to his horse, knowing his work for the day was done.

25

Passin could see the enormous mountain directly ahead of him, the final destination, the passageway that would lead to death and despair for his son and his family. But where did it lead him? To a place where the memories of his son, his first born son, his heir who would bring greatness to the name Barina far beyond what even Saerphin had ever managed, would be evaporated? Would the Dark Lord Saritin eventually be the one who could bring him peace, or was he sacrificing his last remaining child for an empty promise, one man's dream which would transform into his nightmare.

One of his fellow Acolytes, Machillas, the taller of the two abductors, was sat next to him in the front of the cart. By this point they were confident that Zanati posed no threat of escape, a day's ride without food or the room to move ones legs would deprive any man of the Empire of their ability to force an escape, let alone an eight year old who had no idea who he had been taken by, why he had been taken or where he was being taken to. By this point Zanati was

probably too scared and weary to contemplate running even if they threw him out of the cart.
"We're getting near, good, I can't take any more of this forsaken journey. The heat is too much, why doesn't it just hurry up and rain already" Machillas lamented, his dark eyes fixed on the dark clouds above as though he could magically force them to open and relief him of his discomfort.

Dark clouds had been hovering overhead all day, but there was still no relief from the sweltering heat, which seemed to be made worse by the impending storm. The air was close, the conditions humid to the point both men felt as though they had been wrapped in several layers of wool and placed upon a pyre. Saerphin had tried avoiding conversation as much as possible, his mind too distracted by the situation, but it had been largely unavoidable.

"Not long to go now. We'll only be able to ride until the ridge up there though," Passin nodded upwards, in the direction of an area roughly 300 feet up the mountains path, "it becomes too steep for the horses above there, we'll have to get out and climb."

Machillas looked at Passin as though he had just morphed into Saritin himself. The cave where the Saritins Acolytes held their rituals was only three hundred feet off the ground, high enough to kill a man if he fell, but not high enough that it would hurt too much to climb. Machillas, as well as most of the Acolytes, had never climbed higher than that, had never had any need to. "Climb. I wasn't told anything about climbing to the top, this is the highest mountain in the world. This stretches up into the fake God's chambers, and we're meant to climb it. With a hostage as well. We'll never make it!"

Passin was growing weary of the man's whining. "Well, you don't have to, you can stay down here if you like. Suffer the same fate as the rest of the Empire when Saritin descends and condemns the believers of the fake God. It's completely your choice, but I know where I'm going to be. I've waited too long for this night to let a mountain climb stand in my way, regardless of how large and how steep. I'll keep walking until my legs can carry me no more."

Machillas did not have a reply, and so instead grew quiet. He was not happy with developments, but knew better than to make too much of it. Even if tonight was not the night Saritin ascended upon earth, he did not want to risk Lutander's wrath either, and so instead spent his time staring upwards at the imposing mountain ahead of him, trying his hardest to work out its size. It was beyond what any man had ever been able to calculate.

Passin was not concerned about the size of the mountain, he would do whatever was required. Passin had something completely different to annoyance over a petty inconvenience on his mind. He was feeling an emotion he should not have been, and one he had been trying to push out of his mind all day, guilt. The guilt he had been feeling over his son's predicament had been eating at him, and he had been trying his hardest to block it out, but now he had a new guilt to eat at him, the death of his brother. The death of his brother because of his actions, his decisions.

However much Passin knew Saerphin's death was inevitable, there was always something in him that told him his brother would be too strong for these men, too quick, too clever, too much ability. Passin knew that for the plan to work his brother's death was necessary, there was never any doubt that he would follow as soon as he learnt of Zanati being taken, but that did not make the pain any easier. The anxiety he had been feeling all day, the fear that he would turn around and see the familiar face of Saerphin Barina, should have been replaced with relief, but instead it had been replaced with sheer, uncompromising guilt and shame. His brother had died coming to the aid of his Nephew, Passin's son, the boy who would die because of Passin's actions.

Is the Dark Lord within me already, for me to have committed such evil on this earth? Does he already have control of my soul, has he turned it black and evil?

The deeper Passin got into the plan, the further along he went and the more extreme his actions, the more he felt he was committed to seeing it through to the end. He was stuck in a set of events which he had no control over and which had so much momentum he could not stop it if he had the power of a thousand men. There was no backing out now.

When he had been told by Lutander that his son was the target, the boy Saritin required sacrificed, Passin felt as though the plan would change, had to change. Then it did not, and he found himself part of the plot to kidnap Zanati in plain daylight. For the whole journey from Baerithus to Chiawanga he had assumed that someone, anyone, would stop them, be they some righteous Serintinals, do good Atlantean citizens or, more likely, Saerphin. No Serintinals, no citizens and now, as Prization had just confirmed as he rode past towards the mountain, no Saerphin. The options had dwindled, Passin's opportunity to back out and save Zanati soon disappeared. He was committed to the plan now, completely impotent to prevent the inevitable fate his son was facing.

From the top of the mountain, Lutander could see the cart travelling steadily up the Cartemine Road, Passin in front, progressively transporting their prize to its rightful place - to him. He had never truly trusted Passin, despite the good things he was told of the man. He thought he was weak, easily manipulated and not a true believer in the cause. It seemed he might have judged the man too soon.

Lutander had assumed Passin would change his mind, realize the horrific nature of the task given to him and try to allow his son to escape. Sending him on the journey had been a test, to assess whether he really was of the mantle to be embraced by Saritin. He had passed the test, although there was never any risk that if he had not they would lose their prize. The Acolytes Lutander had sent with Passin on the journey had been told to keep an eye on the man, and open his throat should he show any sign of weakness. For all of Lutander's life, people had assumed he was a weak man, equally as impotent as he thought Passin. They had doubted his ability to elicit change and bring about transformations, but they would see. As they burned in the flames of retribution that were about to envelop this entire Empire, they would see their mistake. For their crimes, for worshipping the fake God *Toral* and doubting the power of the True God *Saritin*, and the true strength of Lutander, they would see his power. They would see him transform from a man to a demon, from mortal to invincible, from the man they had treated with contempt to the last thing they would ever see.

With the hour approaching sunset, an eerie shadow had been cast upon the Empire. Lutander could see for miles and miles from the mountain top, from the gusty oceans to the overcrowded villages, from the calm countryside to the magnificence of the Empirical Palace. The sun was gradually coming closer to setting, which would bring about the last light the people of this Empire would ever see. Lutander looked from this view to the sky above, and for the first time that day, a loud crackle of thunder gave the dark clouds permission to release their cold, liquid captives. As the wet soaked through to Lutanders skin he smiled, all was in place, and nothing could stop him now.

26

Unsure whether he had been awoken by the soft, ritualistic chant emulating from the strange woman in front of him, or the overpowering scent of honey mixed with lemon and oregano which was gradually forcing its way unopposed into his nostrils, so sweet yet so intoxicating, or the scattering of raindrops which made their way through the shelter provided by the tree branches above, Saerphin eventually began to stir. Opening his blood-shot eyes, he drank in his surroundings, saying a private prayer to The *Great Lord Toral* that he was seeing anything at all, he had assumed all was lost the second he had hit the water. The grassy enclave he could see around him told him the *Great Lord* had spared him, perhaps he had more support than he realized.

The woman stopped chanting. "Our great warrior is back amongst us, I see." The woman speaking was elderly and large, with dark black hair and wrinkled, sagging skin. She spoke with the confident tone of someone who was used to being around injured men, and was not fazed by the blood and horror which came from them.

"Who are you." Saerphin croaked. "And where am I?" Even in his state of disorientation, Saerphin knew that he did not recognize the surroundings.

"Good questions, although I will not answer either. I am here because you needed help Saerphin. You were close to death, and I do not allow death, I preserve life, I heal, that is what I do. You, Saerphin, you are a warrior, you fight, you kill, that is what you do. You fight for right, for justice, to protect the people of this great Empire from evil. The fight is not over! I have done my part, now you must continue your journey, there is still much to do, and not much time to do it in."

Saerphin tried sitting up. The pain in his stomach was excruciating, he felt as though his entire midriff was about to rip open whenever he moved. He looked down at the expansive line of stitches which had been weaved across his stomach, almost in a perfect line. *Pain will not stop me, I enjoy pain, embrace it. It is only my body that hurts, there is much more on the line than that.*

The pain had brought a strange sense of purpose into Saerphin, an urgency which sent adrenaline surging through his body. Looking curiously at the strange woman, Saerphin asked "You will not tell me who you are, and where I am, but will you at least tell me where I need to be? I am strong, I am ready to continue my journey, and I will not be stopped again."

"Good." The woman replied. "I see an inner strength in you, a light that will be this Empire's candle, to direct it from the darkness. Our Empire needs you, you are our savior, our salvation. If you climb through those trees, you will be back on the path. I've left the monstrous beast of yours, vicious thing, tied up, you'll

find him, and that sword which failed you this time is here." The woman handed Xinias to Saerphin. "See that he does not fail you again."
Saerphin stared at Xinias for a long moment, glad to have his trusted steel back in his hands. "I will not, you can...."
As Saerphin looked up, the woman was gone. All that was left was the lingering aroma, soft and invigorating.

27

Ajinaxa could see the scout clambering back down the side of the mountain. Now he was on one of the lower slopes, further down than the dangerous steep mountain side he had just climbed, he could move a bit faster, and was rapidly sliding and hopping over any obstacles in front of him, trying his hardest not to slip and fall in the now heavy rain.
Slow down, we do not want them to see you boy.
Ajinaxa had positioned his men to the right of the mountain from the Cartemine Road, away from the vantage point of the Acolytes. Yet even so, he did not want any erratic movements which might catch one of their scout's eyes. The Emperor had been very clear; this boy was to be saved, no matter what. If the Acolytes learnt of Ajinaxa and his Serintinals presence, they would slit the boy's throat in a moment, without thought. Ajinaxa did not accept failure, when he was set a task he completed it regardless of what it took. He had learnt that lesson from his father.

The scout reached him. Providing a quick salute, the nimble young Serintinal panted "Sir, I reached the top, but couldn't get near them. They're camped in good, they've got scouts all over the perimeter. I counted maybe 40 men, there could have been more I couldn't see, but I did see the boy."

Ajinaxa's heart jumped, this is what he wanted to hear. "So he's here, without a doubt?"

"He is, a blonde boy, about eight but small for it, it had to be him. He was tied up, on some sort of rack. I could hear him crying from where I was. I've no idea how long he's got, but I couldn't get anywhere near him. He's got at least five guards around him at all times. I don't know if they're expecting a rescue attempt, but they've sure as hell prepared for one."

That was what Ajinaxa had feared, they would need to approach with tact, not brute force. If they launched an assault on the mountain, and faced these Acolytes head on, the boy would be dead before they got within five hundred yards of him. If that happened, even if they killed every Acolyte present, the mission would still be deemed a failure in the eyes of Emperor Tinithius.

Unacceptable.

"Did you see their leader? Anyone who looked like they might have been in charge?"

"No sir, not that I know of. There was an older man, who seemed to be giving orders, but I wouldn't have said he looked like a leader. He was half the size of the other men there, and looked older than my grandfather."

Lutander. It had to be. Before this day Ajinaxa had never heard the name, but one of the men he had brought with him had knowledge of these Saritins Acolytes, so Ajinaxa had him inform him and the other Serintinals on the Acolytes during the journey over.

They seemed like any ordinary outlaw group, perhaps more extreme, although not much considering some of the groups within the Empire, but the stories told of the leader Lutander intrigued Ajinaxa. No-one knew who this man was, where he was from or even whether he was the man who founded the Acolytes, or whether he had taken over from another. He was to all a ghost, unknown and faceless. Ajinaxa believed in the wisdom of knowing his enemies intimately, it rankled him that he did not even know what this man's real name was, nor what he looked like. The man's unanimity could prove to be a real problem if Emperor Tinithius wanted the man responsible in front of him, and the other Acolytes were resolute in not identifying the man, religious kinds usually were.

Men did not just gain the hearts and souls of so many men coming from nowhere, as a nobody, as Ajinaxa had learnt himself. It had taken him years of hard work, sacrificing all his time, making enemies around every corner, bending to the will of men in superior positions, in order to gain the position of Head Serintinal. This man Lutander did not simply wake up and decide to form this group, he had to have some form of power or influence. He had to be a man people knew, who had turned his back on his Empire for greed and power. And whoever he was, he had personality, he had character, people either liked him, trusted him or were scared of him. That was always the case.

Whoever this man was, he had formed a deadly group and was halfway towards achieving his aim today. Ajinaxa would treat him with the respect he deserved and take the subtle approach. Turning his attention back to the scout in front of him. "The way you climbed, where there any other pathways? Is there any way to the top other than the main path, where we will not be seen?"

The scout contemplated the question for a moment, before a look of realization dawned upon his face. "I know a way."

28

Panitias had never been this far from home in her life. Even the air smelled different, although she could not say whether it was for the better or for the worse, the heavy rain was making the air damp and moist. The rain had been welcome when it had first come, providing a cool relief from the sweltering heat. But now Panitias would have prayed for it to go, as the wet gradually sunk through her tunic, if it were not for the fact she had more important things to pray for.

Sanithia had tried being good company throughout the journey, engaging Panitias in conversation, cracking the occasional joke to try and lighten the mood and relieve some stress, even singing several bawdy songs he had obviously learnt at some tavern or another during his years on this earth. But Panitias was not in the right frame of mind for the mood to be made lighter. She wanted it made dark, as dark as the night sky was about to become, a suffocating darkness which would not be lifted until her child was back in her arms. As the weather became more and more somber, Sanithia had given up trying to engage his travel companion, so both travelled in silence, contemplating the journey ahead.

Looking up as they reached the top of a hilly bend in the road, Panitias jolted in surprise. They had been riding for longer than she knew, and were both tired and lethargic, their energy zapped by the repetitive nature of the journey, freezing cold due to the rain, but now she saw what they had been waiting to see. As her horse began to climb down the slight slope in front of them, she could see the end of the journey, their destination, where she would either get her son back, or never return from. She had been looking straight ahead, with trees to her right, she had not realized when she turned the corner that she would be met the imposing frame of Mount Chiawanga.

Sanithia saw it also, it could not be missed. "I guess I don't need to tell you what that is, huh." The old man shouted, the rain and wind carrying his words in several directions.

Panitias shook her head slowly, mesmerized by the mountain''s sheer size. She had heard tales, but hearing tales from travelers and local men was nothing like seeing this wonder with her own eyes. What stood in front of her could only have been created by *Toral* himself, Panitias prayed that he was present to help her.

Toral and Saerphin, surely no man in the Empire could deny that combination.

Sanithia continued. "I've been here once or twice…on my travels…but I don't know the mountain very well. There's a large path that goes from the bottom to the top, it will be dangerous, very dangerous, especially on a wet night like this, but they'll have taken your son to the peak, I know they will have. We have no choice but to follow."

Dangerous? Panitias thought. *Dangerous is the men that oppose us when we reach the top.* Climbing the mountain was the least of her worries.

Panitias decided against pointing this out, and so simply nodded again. "How long will it take to get to the top?" She yelled over the noise of the wind and rain. "Night is upon us, we will need some form of light to illuminate our path. We don't have the luxury of enough time to travel slow and sure." Panitias glanced again at the old man's missing hand. She was constantly fighting the temptation to speed off and leave him behind, although the thought that his knowledge of the mountain may be of use had so far made her hesitate to do so.

A devilish smirk crossed Sanithias's face, he saw the glance. Ignoring it, he pulled out a wooden torch from inside the woolen bag he had slung around his shoulder. "My father used to tell me, always be prepared. You never know how much will be riding on it."

Panitias was happy to see that Sanithia was being of more use than she thought he would be, although she still had the feeling he was not telling her the truth fully. The bag he was carrying was dyed blue, a surefire sign of wealth, and the torch he carried looked like it had been ornately carved. Where would a preacher without means to gain coin have access to such things? On top of that, his jovial attitude still rankled her; he was clearly enjoying this journey more than she would have liked him too. However, she would need to be certain he would be of no more use before she ditched him; she knew the cost of any little mistake.

Before either of them knew it, they were upon the mountain, reaching the end of the Cartemine Road, which did not have a definite ending but rather the paving below gradually began to fade, until eventually their horses were trotting on nothing but grass. Finally, they reached an impasse where their horses could go no further, the curving path leading up the mountain was far too narrow and treacherous to even consider attempting on horseback.

"I guess we've reached the end of our use for these, huh." Sanithia stated as he hopped off his filly. "I don't know about you, but I'm hungry, we'll need our energy if we're climbing...that!" Sanithia pointed upwards, almost vertically, to the top of the mountain. "What do you say about setting up a fire and cooking one of these? Grilled horse sounds perfect to me, we can ride back with one between us."

As both Panitias and Sanithia looked up, the sheer magnitude of how high they would be climbing hit them both. However, unlike Sanithia, Panitias was driven by urgency, the urgency to reach the mountain peak as soon as possible and save her baby, the maternal instinct that told her she did not need food, she did not need rest, all she needed was to continue, whatever the cost. To allow her motherly strength to drive her forward, and meet any of the obstacles she was about to face head on. Whether it be lack of food, lack of rest, high, slippery mountain climbs or Saritin worshippers with sharp blades, no obstacle would stop her from what she came here to do, no hindrance would be too great to stop her from reaching her child and taking him back home, back where he belonged.

"We've no time, if you want to stop and eat old man, feel free, but I'm going on." Panitias hopped off her horse and began marching up the path, to emphasize the point.

"Fair enough, I'll join you." Sanithia replied. "The flames and smell would probably have alerted someone to our presence anyway. Last thing we want is to be killed before we've even started climbing the mountain."

Panitias glared at Sanithia for that last comment. She was not sure whether she was happy he was continuing with her or not, but she was content in the thought that if she had to ditch him, she could do at a moment's notice. There was no way a cripple could catch her up if she decided to excel her speed up the mountain.

As they walked gradually away from their horses, the undisciplined fillies heaved off, overexcited by the prospect of freedom. Panitias and Sanithia began their trawl up the heavy mud path, each step a struggle, but a struggle which with every step took them slowly closer to their aim.

The short, stocky man in the red mask had been standing guard near the bottom of the mountain since the sun was near enough mid sky, and had not seen anything suspicious, no one entering the mountain who was not meant to be. Not until very recently, when he saw movement in the distance, coming up the Cartemine Road.

Keeping his position, camouflaged within a conveniently positioned bush some hundred yards up the mountain path, the masked man could see a man and a woman ascending on foot. The two new arrivals said nothing to each other, but walked with a purpose, driven by the woman. The masked man did not recognize her, but he recognized the steely look in her eyes, the determined way she walked, the non-compromising pout on her lips. There was only one person this woman could be, although he did not know who the cripple was.

As they neared his position, the masked man knew what he had to do, however little he relished the prospect. In a previous life he had been a proud man,

a man who had believed himself noble, a man who believed himself respected and worthy of respect.
What kind of respected man kills a woman and a cripple in an ambush, without even showing his face?
The nagging sense of shame, the feeling that he was better than his actions were about to prove, were too much for the masked man. The woman and the cripple had to die, he did not doubt that, but their death did not need to bring him shame. He was killing in the name of *Saritin*, the One True God; he would not be seen as a coward.
Just before the man and the woman reached him, the masked man jumped out into the path before them, causing both to jolt in surprise. Surprise turned to fear as they saw the large sword in his hand, and the masked man became the non-masked man, pulling the fraying material from over his head and revealing a squat, freckled face, a face which would have been unthreatening in many scenarios, but which looked like evil personified in this one.

Panitias had expected someone to stop them from reaching the top, but she had not expected someone this low, barely a few hundred feet into the climb. Her heart was racing as she stood just five feet away from this unsuspected assailant, so close she could smell the sweaty, unwashed fabric of his clothes, even the wine on his breath. With his ordinary looking face, she would never have taken him for one of the animals she was here to face. Yet here she was, face to face with one of the men who had taken her child.
"You both came to the wrong place tonight. I'll allow you to pull your weapons, to make this a fair fight, but I'm afraid I can't let you leave. I can't allow anything to stop tonight, when the *One True God* descends upon this earth and takes his rightful place."

Sanithia was frozen in fear, he looked like he had never faced a situation such as this before. Panitias had not either, although her fear was overtaken by her maternal instinct. *If this man kills me now, I cannot save Zanati.*
Panitias had no weapon but her cunning, which she intended to use to its fullest. "You can't slay a woman and a cripple without allowing them to at least try and defend themselves, what kind of man would allow himself to do that? We have no weapons, provide us some if you intend to kill us with honor. If not, then slay us like an animal, like a coward with no balls, unwilling to face combat like a man?" Panitias knew enough about the male psyche to know her taunts would strike a nerve, and without fail the man's response told her she had succeeded, as he withdrew a blade which had been hidden in his belt and carelessly threw it to her feet.
"I only have the one, decide between you which of you has the pleasure to use it. Makes no difference to me, the result will be the same."
Panitias glanced sideways at Sanithia, whose face had gone a disconcerting shade of white, whiter than the wool of fresh shaven sheep in the farmlands. His whole body was violently shaking, as though some unseen presence had him gripped by the shoulders and was seeing if it could make the old man's head fall off. Sanithias reaction told Panitias all she needed to know of which of them would need to be taking charge if they were to stand any chance of surviving the situation.
"You know, whatever you do to me now doesn't matter. Saerphin Barina, the greatest warrior this Empire has ever known, is the boy's uncle. He'll be on his way up the mountain as we speak, ready to strike down your evil brothers and save my child. You may

as well leave now, and I'll tell him you had nothing to do with any of this."

Panitias prayed this man would hold enough fear of Saerphin's legend to be intimidated by her words. "If I were you, I'd leave now, before he finds you."

The man grinned, a dangerous grin with a gleam of menace in his eyes. "Saerphins dead, lady. Slain by Prization, the *true* greatest warrior this Empires ever seen. I heard it from the big man's own mouth, he's up the mountain himself. Besides, even if he wasn't, I heard he was nothing but a drunk nowadays anyway, a degenerate alcoholic who sells his sword for coin. From what I've heard, I could probably take him myself." The grin was now smug and self satisfied. "Give up any thoughts of survival, there shall be no saving of the child, and there shall be no saving of you."

The words hit Panitias like a brick thrust into her midriff, taking all the air from her body. She could not speak, she could not react. Now she knew, she was the only one who could save Zanati.

Slowly bending down, she grabbed the blade from the ground, her eyes not leaving the man in front of her. She envisioned what she intended to do, where she intended to strike, how she was going to best this man. She had never fought anyone in her life, let alone with a weapon, and did not have a clue where she would start. She did not know how she could stand a chance to win if she had the same or even a larger blade than her opponent, but with a blade at least half a foot shorter than the mammoth sword he held, she contemplated whether turning to run would be the more prudent idea.

Turn, and this man won't think twice about wedging that sword between your shoulder blades. These are evil men, men without honor.

As soon as Panitias was stood upright, with the blade in her hand, the man descended upon her. Circling Panitias, then going back the way he came, all the while keeping an eye on Sanithia on the off chance he had an injection of bravery, he was clearly weighing up his best method of attack.

Prowl left, prowl right. Prowl left, prowl right. Prowl left, prowl right. Prowl left, prowl right. Prowl left, prowl right.

The man finally struck.

His movements were far from lightning fast, and Panitias jumped out of the sword's path, her heart racing frantically as she felt the momentum created by the wind swooshing where her body had been just half a second earlier. This man appeared unconcerned with bringing his best performance, confident that he could slay both opponents without exerting himself too much. It would be a long night, and he would no doubt want as much energy as possible when the showcase was reached. Panitias knew the man's tactics were right, he did not need to perform to his fullest to see off his current opponents.

Panitias did not know exactly what the best move to do was, but she knew she had to do something. Standing there and allowing this man to attack her was suicide, an offensive plan was a must. She swung the blade towards the man, but he jumped out the way. Her body was left exposed, but he did not strike. Panitias could not tell whether he was weary or arrogant, the man's face was neutral, expressionless. She tried again, missing again, but this time he did strike her. A firm connection with the back of his hand sent her sprawling, the blade flying out of her hand in the opposite direction. When her head cleared of the haze created by the blow, Panitias was on the floor, her back against a tree, completely exposed. She could see the man, standing above her, his sword hanging contently just above her throat.

"You shouldn't have come here tonight. I gave you a chance, but I can do no more for you." The man's tone seemed almost regretful.

Panitias looked to her right, where Sanithia stood in the exact same spot as before, the same helpless look on his face. *Some use you were, old man.*

Panitias knew that her options were at an end, and her fate was sealed. Her anguish that she would not be able to save her son was unbearable, her only solace that her pain would be over in a few moments, ended with one swift strike from the sword which was so close to her face it was almost shaving her.

Panitias couldn't take her eyes off the long sword, the sharp blade, the way the rain bounced off the glistening steel. Panitias said her final prayers as the man pulled sword back sideways, preparing to land the fatal chop, when Panitias saw a different blade. A smaller blade, but one that looked sharper, creeping around the man's neck. Before he could react, the blade had been sliced efficiently across his jugular, which instantly spurted a thick, juicy liquid all over Panitias, a final gasp of air struggled from the shocked looking face above her.

As the dead man crumbled to the floor in a lifeless heap, Panitias was greeted with the heart soaring image of Saerphin standing just behind, wiping the blood from Xinias on the back of the corpse's tunic. She had never been so happy to see him in her life.

29

No man present knew whether the image in the flame was good or bad, to be rejoiced or renounced, the saving of their Empire or leading it to its doom. The wise old men present had seen many things in their time, combined and individually, but they had never seen an Empire's fate resting upon such thin margins. The Empire's salvation was certainly still possible, not probable, that had been debated all day by these wise old man. The debate continued.
"We should be doing something?" Jarib declared, as the flames began to die out. "The fate of the entire Empire rests upon tonight, and we are sitting here doing nothing." Throughout the day Jarib had been anxious, and this anxiety had led to several outbursts of frustration. Siphorious knew better than to goad his fellow Angel.
"My brother, our *Great Lord Toral* is the one who is truly in charge of the situation, regardless of what others may believe. They are merely pawns in *His* plan. He has set the Empire a test today, and if we fail, then the fate of the Empire is as *He* sees fit. It is

not our place to interfere anymore than we have, which is probably already too much." Siphorious had been wrestling with his conscience all day, debating whether he had been right to alert Saerphin to the dangers his Nephew was in. *Was that what the Great Lord Toral wanted?*

"All we can do is stay here and pray." Siphorious' continued. His voice had a calming and neutral effect, few found themselves able to argue with it. However, Jarib had known the man long enough not to let his voice's cooling effects work on him, and continued to argue his point.

"We have stayed here and prayed all day, yet the boy is still atop that mountain, surrounded by monsters."

"Monsters of *our* creation" Tarinthium intersected. "We have failed in our duties as the moral compass of this Empire, as much as any of the rulers or the people. Today, we are being judged by *Toral* as much as anyone, and if the monsters we allowed to thrive succeed, then we deserve the fate that awaits us as much as anyone, however painful that is to hear."

All four men were quiet at that, contemplating the validity of the words. Finally, Matasinthius spoke. Normally the quietest of the Angels, Matasinthius was full of wisdom, and when he spoke the others listened. Siphorious may have been the unofficial leader, yet Matasinthius was the Angel whose words were greatest heeded.

"My brothers, we are all confused, all anxious, all even a little scared, I will not deny that. I thought I had seen all that was to be seen within my lifetime, yet I was clearly wrong. I too, such as my brother Jarib here, have the temptation to act, to intersect myself and assist however I can, however frail my aged body may be." Matasinthius looked down at his decrepit frame as if to emphasize the point.

"Yet in the end, the words of brother Siphorious are true. We are not men of action, we are men of contemplations, men who act as Sheppards with the job of guiding His flock to the eternal paradise. We are His Angels, yet it appears our moral compass was found a-slumber when needed, guiding His ships to a fiery collision with the jagged rocks that are Saritins pit of eternal damnation, instead of directing them to His glorious presence. Tonight is the Empire's chance at redemption, to save themselves from the fate that their actions, and our lack of actions, have brought upon them. All we can do is pray."

All four men's eyes returned to the flames, with hope in their hearts, but trepidation in their minds.

30

The embrace between Saerphin and Panitias was long and emotion fuelled, Panitias squeezing so tightly a smaller man might have received broken ribs, her sobs intermittent and powerful. Eventually, they departed the clinch.
"Saerphin, I thought you were dead." Panitias managed through her tears. "But you're here, you're here to save my baby. Zanati still had a chance."
Saerphin nodded. "I thought I was dead too. Who's this…" Saerphin had not had a chance to look at the man standing to the side, deathly white and shaking uncontrollably. Now he did see him, the words went from him, leaving him speechless and bewildered.
"This is Sanithia" Panitias replied, in her euphoria to still be alive and on her way to way save her child not picking up on Saerphin's confusion.
"Sanithia, you say." Saerphin eyed the man coolly.
"Yes, my name is Sanithia." The old man struggled his reply, extending the hand he still had to Saerphin, but receiving no hand in return.

"Do you know who I am...*Sanithia?*" Saerphin glared at the man, leaving no illusion about whether the ruse was still applicable. The familiar face he had seen at a glance in the market, it only just hit him. The old man stumbled a reply. "You are Saerphin...I...I...I've heard of you, you're a great warrior, a great Atlantean, you were a great Serintinal."

Saerphin snorted in derision. "I was a great Serintinal; I was a less great Head Serintinal, until I walked away. Do you know why I walked away....Emperor Jhaerin?"

The look on Jhaerin's face would have confirmed his statement even if Saerphin had not been completely certain, which he had been, he had seen that face enough in court during his time as Head Serintinal, but the sigh of shock which came from Panitias displayed her surprise.

"Saerphin, what do you mean? This is a crippled preacher from the Baerithus market who's come to help me today, he cannot be Emperor Jhaerin. Emperor Jhaerin is dead, everyone knows that. Some whore cut his throat when he was asleep."

"I'm dead too, don't you remember." Saerphin had not taken his eyes off Jhaerin since he had made the recognition. That face he had despised for so much time. The man who could have stopped the Acolytes so long ago, the man who had allowed corruption and evil to spread within the Empire until it was unstoppable. Now he was standing face to face with him, sword in hand, and no idea why he was here.

Jhaerin started to respond. "Look, I know this is a strange situation, but I came here to help. Your brother's wife needed help, and I'm here to provide it."

"Some help you were when I was about to have my throat sliced open." Panitias hissed in reply. "You lied to me, I knew you were lying, but I didn't know why. Is that why you're here, to hand me to those monsters when we get to the top. Are you the one who's going to kill my baby?" Panitias started pounding her fists on Jhaerins chest, with enough force to cause the old man to stumble backwards, tripping on a tree and falling onto his backside.

As much as Saerphin wanted to join Panitias in beating the man, he knew they needed answers first. "Panitias, there will be time for that later." He said as he took her by the shoulders and directed her away from the fallen old man. With Panitias out of the way, Saerphin stood over the former most powerful man in the Empire, Xinias unsheathed, and placed the razor sharp blade to the old man's throat.

"Now I want you to tell me the truth, or so help me, in the name of *Toral,* they won't be telling lies when they say Emperor Jhaerin had his throat slit wide open." Saerphin growled at the old man, nearly a year's worth of hatred and venom present in his voice. "Why are you here? What is your plan?"

Jhaerin stuttered his response again, squirming away from the fear inspiring presence of the blades tip wherever he could.

"I'm here to help. I walked away from power, I'm not Emperor any more, my son , Tinithius is, he is a good boy, he'll make a good Emperor, better than I ever did. I want to help my people, and the boy needed helping. I swear, there is no other motive."

"I'm not here to hear about your son." Saerphin hissed.

"Ok, I'll tell you why I'm here. I had a dream. A dream of the future of the Empire, the fate that awaits us if we do not change our ways and follow the teachings of The *Great Lord Toral.* The Empire has become corrupted…"

"Is that meant to be news?" Saerphin growled.
"Of course not, the point is unless we repent, then we'll be destined to damnation. The boy tonight, I think it's a test, to see whether we are saveable. If the boy dies, so does the Empire."
Saerphin snorted in reply. "You really believe that old man?"
"I do, with all my heart and soul. I am here to help save the boy, to make amends for all the evil I allowed to enter this Empire, and to save us from damnation." Saerphin could not deny, the man spoke with conviction and sincerity. *He's a trained liar, that's what they teach them from birth in the palace. Don't listen to a word of it.*
"Please," Jhaerin continued, "Let me help you save the boy. The Empire needs it."
Saerphin looked at Panitias, who had been trying her hardest to take this new information in. "Do you believe him?"
Panitias thought for a moment. "I don't know. I've had the sense he was lying, but in truth I haven't had the sense he was lying for un-noble reasons. His argument does make sense, and so far he hasn't let me down, not including his statue act when we were ambushed."
Jhaerin intersected. "I know a secret path, up the mountain. Few know of it. I had it made especially so I could reach the top of the mountain whenever I liked when I was in the area without being troubled by anyone on the way up. I'm pretty sure the men who made it were killed afterwards, so they could not reveal the location of the path to anyone." Saerphin drew his blade closer to Jhaerins throat to show his disgust at the story.
"Look, I regret that as much as you and I'm as responsible as the man who did the deed by my lack

of action, but I'm here trying to make up for it. If you try and take the central path, they'll see you coming, and even with your fighting skills you won't stand a chance against the amount of men they'll have up there. If you take me with you, I'll show you the secret path."

Saerphin thought for a long moment. His initial temptation was to open the liar's throat and be done with it, but the man had a point about the mountain. Jhaerin did not know any way up other than the main path, which would be beset with ambushes, and even if they survived them, if the men at the peak saw him ascending, they would kill Zanati in a moment's notice. As little as Saerphin liked it, this man may be essential to their plan.

"I'm going to tell you now, and I'm only going to say it once. We don't have time to waste, if I see you doing anything strange, if I even get a strange feeling in my bones that you're going to turn on us, you're going over the mountain edge. Do you understand?"

Jhaerin nodded earnestly.

"Then let's go, we don't have much time, direct us to this secret path." Saerphin grabbed Jhaerin by the collar and hauled him to his feet. As Jhaerin began leading the way, Saerphin and Panitias shared an uneasy glance. *Are we getting into bed with Saritin himself?*

31

"It's there! I can see it! I can see home! Oh joyous Atlantis, how I've missed you! "
The sun was almost completely down, but through the near darkness, Gurain could see the light at the end of the journey, the shores of Atlantis lit as always by the Sea Protectors large, unmistakable lights. It had been a long time since Gurain had cried, but at that moment he could not hold back the tears, which within seconds were streaming down his face, mixing with the heavy rain drops and becoming salty by the time they reached his mouth. Tears of joy, tears of relief. As he looked around, he could see that he was not alone. The usually macho environment of the ship's hull was transformed into streams of grown men sobbing in relief, they would have a chance to see home again. The relief was evident in all, except one man.
"Blast you all to the *Great Lord,* stop that pathetic blubbering, all of you. There's enough water in the sea, already, do you want to make our journey harder? " Gurain was unsure whether this was meant

to be a joke, but one look at Cronias, who was glaring across the decks without a hint of emotion on his face told him, unsurprisingly for the stern captain, that he was not. "In case you emotional women had not noticed, there's still a Greek naval fleet behind us, and they're still chasing us at a very fast speed. If you keep crying instead of rowing, you won't reach anywhere, and you certainly won't be seeing your families again. Now get your oars back in your lazy work avoiding hands, and row like your life depends upon it. Because believe you me, it still does. And I'm not dying at the hands of them Greek bastards because you all got emotional and teary."

As much as he hated to admit it, Gurain knew that the captain was right. If they took it easy and didn't give every last drop of energy into rowing, the Greeks could, probably would, still catch them, and all their effort would be for nothing.

Even worse. Might they decide to keep going? That once they've destroyed our naval fleet, Atlantis is ripe for the taking? I cannot allow my family to become Greek slaves. I have seen firsthand the horrors that become of such people.

Gurain had the oar back in his hands, and felt that familiar pain in his shoulder once again as he commenced rowing. But this time instead of resenting the pain, he embraced it, rejoiced in its purity, celebrated the fact that each second he felt that pain was a second he was closer to home, and now he could see those familiar shores he was sure of that fact. He did not take his eyes off them, for fear that they may be a mirage, a figment of his exhausted and dehydrated imagination, and that if he looked away he would never see them again. The shores of Atlantis had never seemed so beautiful, so inviting.

Gurains pride and manhood, the same as those of his fellow warriors, had been diminished when forced to retreat from their enemy. That he had been strong enough to survive, to keep rowing in the face of excruciating pain, to dig deep and refuse to surrender, had brought back some of that pride. He had done what was required to ensure that, even if the Greeks did reach Atlantis, that he would be there to face them front on, on home advantage, and ensure they did not take his home.

I will not allow them to do that! If it takes my dying breath to prevent it, I cannot allow that to happen!

32

An endless stream of clouds were completely covering the moon, preventing all light from escaping and creating an eerie darkness upon the mountain. Despite the rain the night was quiet, the mood somber. The rain had been gradually becoming stronger as the three would be rescuers got further up the mountain, lashing down upon all with nothing but shallow tree limbs to protect them from its unrelenting assault.
Saerphin and his cohort had struggled up the mountain, against odds of steep, slippery paths, and bar a few slips and scrapes had made it to the top of the mountain without injury. An especially impressive feat considering Jhaerins disability. Now, as they stood just below the mountains peek, they knew they had some decisions to make. One wrong move and Zanati was dead, assuming he was not already.
"We've got to get close, close enough that we can get an outlay of where they are, but not close enough that there's a risk anyone can see us." Saerphin whispered as he peaked up over the mountain's

edge. They had ascended from the secret path upon a huddle of trees, which they had half climbed through in order to gain their current vantage point.

"How do we do that?" Jhaerin replied, his soft voice almost lost in the wind. "If we all go climbing over there, one of us is bound to be seen."

Saerphin thought for a second. As much as he hated that it had come to this situation, he knew the old man was right. Saerphin would have to scout the situation himself, and in doing so leave Panitias with the ex-Emperor.

Saerphin knew that Panitias had travelled with Jhaerin this far and even believed that his story for why he had come was half plausible. But even so, he could not completely discount the theory that the old man was part of the plan, aimed at luring Panitias and, more importantly in the Acolytes eyes, Saerphin out if they got near to rescuing the boy.

The old man had abused his power all his reign, where had this sudden conscience come from? He had had the power to stop the Acolytes whenever he liked, why hadn't he if he was truly against them?

Saerphin knew he had a decision to make.

One wrong move!

The options available to him were not as he would have liked, but he could not change the circumstances he had been given, and he knew in reality if Jhaerin was working against them, their chances were almost non-existent anyway. His only other option was to open Jhaerin's throat here and now, but he would not, could not bring himself to do that, not whilst there was still a chance he could be of use.

Would they take him as trade? Surely the former most powerful man in the Empire is a greater sacrifice to Saritin than a child?

Finally looking back to Jhaerin and Panitias, Saerphin sighed. "We don't have much of a choice here, we need to get close, but above all else we can't afford to be seen. I'm going to go myself, get close, and bring you back what I find. Stay still and silent here."
The frustrated looked on Panitia's face told both men exactly how displeased she was with this plan. "Saerphin, I can understand *his* caution," she looked at Jhaerin with disgust, "but you're a great warrior, far greater than any of those monsters out there. We don't have time for scouting missions, we're going to have to do something soon."
Saerphin looked back at his sister-in-law with shame.
Not better than all of them.
He put his hand to the still raw wound that was festering on his stomach even as they spoke. It itched and irritated as the puss wept from the wound, a constant reminder that he had been bettered, that afternoon, by another man in the Empire.
I will not show fear, I fear no one. If Prization is upon this mountain, he shall feel my blade penetrating his heart the same as any other man present.
Even with this forced confidence, Saerphin had learnt a long time ago the difference between self belief and arrogance. He believed he could best the Acolytes and retrieve his Nephew, but he knew he would need to use his head to do so, not rely solely on brute force.
"I know how you feel Panitias, but believe me when I say, if we go in without a plan, without even knowing where Zanati is, it's suicide, and he'll be dead shortly after us."
Panitias shuddered at the mention of her son's death. Reluctantly, she nodded, all her trust was now placed in her husband's brother.
Where is my brother in her time of need?

"I'll look after Panitias here until you get back." Jhaerin said. Panitias and Saerphin shared a look of doubt, before Saerphin turned, squatted low and began climbing out of the trees, on his front crawling as he reached the wet, muddy grass.

"Be quick, you know what's riding on this!" Panitias called after him as he crawled away.

33

The art of hunting all comes down to the ability to camouflage one's self into any situation, to the point one becomes not just part of the scenery, but the scenery itself. If one were to leave the scenery, one's prey would say something is amiss, and become alarmed. Until one can camouflage into scenery with this level of skill, they can never call themselves an expert hunter, nor expect to catch more than which gets away.

Pragil had been taught that by his father from a young age, and to this day adhered to the principle religiously. As he watched the woman and the cripple, he knew they could not see him, could not hear him, could not smell him, could not sense him. They had absolutely no idea they were even being watched, even though he was only ten yards away from them, close enough to smell the stench of desperation on the woman, the fear that clung to the man like a baby to its mother's breast. Smell was as important as sight when hunting, no matter what the prey, and instinct was most important of all. His instinct told him these were easy prey, their instincts told them nothing at all. That lack of instinct was about to get them killed. The closer Pragil got, the greater the rush. *Would they sense him when he was five yards away? Three yards? One yard? Would it take him to jump upon them like death itself for them to realize their time was up, their plan thwarted and the child's chances of survival gone.* Pragil did not care how long it took, he loved the thrill of the hunt too much to give himself away too early. He could stalk prey like this all day if the circumstances permitted, this was what he lived for.

Pragils heart sank. Out of the corner of his eye, he saw two men, half crouched down, staring right in the direction of *his* prey, their slack movements making them out for amateurs at first sight.

You imbeciles. You're making too much noise; you're not condensing your bodies. You'll be seen in no time. He winced as he heard the clear crackle made by one of the men stepping on a group of twigs, although luckily his prey did not pick up on the sound.

The would be hunters could not see him, a mere three foot behind his prey now, and his prey were either too naïve or stupid to even be keeping an eye out for predators, so did not see the two in front of them, nor sense him behind. If it were not for the fact Pragil took hunting so seriously he would have found the situation comical, as it was he found it excruciatingly frustrating. He did not like being rushed, haste was the enemy of the hunter, yet he saw no further options. He could not savor the moment any longer, every ounce of pleasure he would get from this hunt had now been squeezed out, he would need to pounce now in order to claim the victims his own.

He was now close enough to touch, his finger tips gently caressed the hairs on the back of the woman's neck, which were standing on end due to the cold. His fingers were the width of an eye lash away from touching the woman's cold, soft skin, yet she still did not know he was there, completely ignorant to his presence and the danger he presented, like a mouse about to be swooped upon and devoured by an owl, she would not know he was there until it was too late. But the fun was over, the hunt was up, if he did not act now the two fools creeping as if they knew how to hunt would take at least some of his credit. *He could not allow that.*

It is a myth that hunters hunt better in packs. Hunters are in it for the glory, the thrill of the chase. This never tastes better than when tasted solitarily, knowing that one's own abilities were the only factor in the success of the hunt, without others attempting to steal the glory.

Lifting the stealthy blade that was firmly gripped in his left hand, Pragil drew the blade in front of the woman's throat in one agile movement, quick as a flash of lightning, and grabbed the back of her flowing hair, yanking her head backwards and exposing his blade to the centre of her neck, elevated inches from her bare jugular. The woman yelped, and the crippled old man's eyes went wide open in shock. He looked as though he had seen a ghost, a pathetic whimper leaving his throat. He knew the game was up.

"Don't move, unless you want her blood all over your pretty tunic!" Pragil hissed. He knew from experience that once caught intimidation was the best way to keep one prey in check, when the prey was human of course. The threat usually eliminated the need for the act, there was as much power in the words as there were in the action.

The man did not look dangerous, yet Pragil knew that appearances could be deceptive. The hunter in him knew to take every situation as though anything could happen, and so prepared thusly. For all he knew, this scared looking cripple was a master one handed swordsman capable of killing them all, should he give him the opportunity. Pragil was sure he had heard myths of such men in his youth.

"Calm down my son, put the blade down and we can talk." The man did not seem to be capable of anything further than whimpering, even when he spoke it was as a whimper, yet Pragil did not lower the blade one inch.

"What do you want to talk about, old man? Whatever it is, you can come and talk to my brothers about it as well."

By now, the two would be hunters were upon them, having seen the commotion caused by his ambush.

"How long have you been there?" The first of the men to arrive questioned, a chubby man, red faced and out of breath from his short sprint.

"Not as long as I'd have liked. Easy prey these two, like plucking baby pigeons from their mothers nest. Don't think you're getting any credit for the catch though, this is all on me. Grab that one, and let's take them to the others, see what they make of our new guests. See if they'll let them stay for the party."

Saerphin had journeyed to the edge of the Acolytes camp, and was now perched half way up a Laurel tree, stealthily camouflaged behind various branches trying to create a mental map of the key points in front of him. The wind on top of the mountain was strong at the best of times, but the impending storm made the wind even more formidable, forcing Saerphin to utilize more of his strength and energy into keeping a grip on the trees flimsy branches than he would have liked. The higher he climbed, the stronger the branches and the greater the view, but the greater the wind, which at this point was forcibly smacking him across the face to the point it brought wetness to his eyes, somewhat hindering his vision.

In front of him he could make out several Acolytes patrolling, a mere 10 foot from his current position. He had chosen this tree as his vantage point as it showed what he had thought was the whole of the central area atop the mountain, yet now he realized that there were several areas still out of site, and clearly his Nephew was in one of these. He could not see any trace of Zanati wherever he looked within the camp, which worried him greatly.

A sudden commotion caught Saerphin's attention from the left, and looking over he saw several excited looking Acolytes marching with pride across the centre of the mountain top, smug looks across their faces. Saerphin's heart dropped when he saw behind them were two prisoners, clearly a man and a woman, who had been forced to wear black hoods, wrapped tightly around their necks. Saerphin did not need to see the missing hand of the man to know the identities of the two prisoners.

I knew I should never have left them.

This complicated Saerphin's task beyond a doubt.

What's the priority now? Save my nephew, or save my sister in law?

Every ounce of his predatory instinct told Saerphin that within this disaster was an opportunity, that if they were distracted with the mother they would be less focused upon the child, yet he could not allow himself to adopt this mindset. However much he wanted to take Zanati back alive, he would not sacrifice attempting to save Panitias for it. Saerphin knew a decision of what action to take was required, and he knew very well the cost of making the wrong one.

 Lutander walked to the centre of the mountain top, the content look upon his face hidden by the red mask he wore.
Three prisoners for the price of one, Lutander truly is blessing us tonight.
"Unmask them, I want to see their faces. And bring the child as well," he commanded. His men obeyed immediately, two aggressively tugging the fabric from over the captive's heads whilst another went to retrieve Zanati, dragging him to the left of the woman, who sobbed uncontrollably as she stared at the child, as though she had seen a ghost.
Not too hard to tell who you are, sweetheart.
Looking across the faces of the three prisoners, Lutander knew that pleasure did not come much greater than this.
Three human beings who are truly and utterly at my will, their fate resting upon my whims, their destiny in my hands. Whether they live or die is based upon whether I command it or not.
Lutander spent a good few seconds staring at the quivering wreck that was the former Emperor of Atlantis.
I am in control of the fate of the former most powerful man in this entire Empire, this is true power.
After appraising all three captives for a long moment, absorbing the feeling of strength, becoming aroused by their helplessness and complete reliance upon him, Lutander spoke, directing the words at his unexpected new prizes.
"You do not know why you are here, and that does not matter. The boy is what matters to us, you should

not have come to retrieve him. You cannot stop the unstoppable, as this Empire is about to discover. The *True* God Saritin is about to descend upon us, and that cannot be stopped, regardless of whatever you had planned."

The woman tried speaking, but her mouth had been gagged tightly, so that all that came out was an illegible mumble. He admired the look of strength in her eyes, the unflinching anger aimed solely at him, yet for all his admiration, what he truly felt was excitement.

Hate me. Loathe me. Wish death upon me. I am in control here. I have the power, am I am strong, so strong. Nothing can stop me.

After a lifetime of being treated as weak, of being laughed at, dismissed and emasculated, Lutander was savoring this feeling, the feeling of strength, the allure of power.

They will never laugh at me again.

"Don't try and speak, your words would have no impact anyway. You have come here today to be heroes, yet you are about to discover the fate which awaits heroes in the true world, this is not a myth to be told to children as they sip their warm milk in the evening. This is reality, what Atlantis is, and what we are about to become. Men would have called me mad if I were to unveil my plans in open, yet I am here now, about to transcend from mortal to immortal, man to a legend. This is about to be the face of an entity greater than you have ever seen. Only the *True* God *Saritin* shall be greater than me."

As Lutander slowly pulled the mask from his face, the stunned gasp which left the ex-Emperors mouth was almost completely masked by the gag, yet Lutander enjoyed the stunned look in his eyes just as much. It was not every day you got to surprise an Emperor to the point he could speak no longer.

The man who had just unmasked himself looked vaguely familiar to Saerphin, yet he could not place where he had seen him before. Did he work in the markets? In the courts? Was he a Serintinal? Saerphin had no clue who the man was, but what he had noticed more than the identity of the masked man was the reaction of Jhaerin. His face had been overcome by a look of complete and utter shock, as though he had seen a ghost rise from the dead. Whoever this man was, Jhaerin knew him well, and was surprised to see him.

Saerphin gave up trying to identify the man, he knew it was a waste of time and that he was not here to play such games. Whoever the man was was unimportant, all that mattered was that the man was stopped. Without time for further plans, Saerphin knew the time to act was now, lest he miss his opportunity.

Avyon. The soft, sweet priest, how can this be? The man the other priests call Grandfather, due to his gentle nature? Can this be the man that stands before me, demonic and forsaken, possessed by a force so dark it would allow a child to be murdered in cold blood?

Jhaerin felt as though he had been struck in the stomach with the mountain itself. He had said as little words to Avyon as possible in his whole life, had never seen much reason to speak to the priest. He knew he was well respected by many of his fellow priests, and generally manipulated by the others. What he had achieved, his personality, his demeanor, all of it made the concept that he could be the cause behind this situation seem utterly implausible to Jhaerin.

Am I having another dream? At what point will I awake back in my Palace chambers, hung over and cranky? Will Avyon be the one to bring me honeyed tea to quell the headache?

The vicious cold rain smacking straight into Jhaerin's face told him that this was not a dream, yet he could not shake the sense of surreal that had overcome him.

Avyon, or the man Jhaerin knew as Avyon, had his eyes fixed solely on Jhaerin, reading him, drinking in the look of unadulterated shock which was still paralyzing, stopping him from speaking, stopping him from even being able to fully process the situation.

"Emperor Jhaerin, my how you've changed. I'm sure I remember you having two hands?" Lutander could not stop smirking as he spoke. "Tell me, do you remember the amount of times I brought you another drink when you were too drunk to get one yourself, as though I was a serving boy? Do you remember the times I was sent to the city brothels to find you a whore for the night? Do you remember the early morning prayers you were meant to attend, but were too hung over to get out of bed? I forgave you for them all did I not? You look positively shocked, was I not the person you were expecting to see here today?"

Jhaerin could not respond verbally, for reasons beyond the gag, but he managed a weak shake of the head.

This man's soul is broken and crushed. Lutander smirked. "Well I am the man standing in front of you today, the man in control. This Empire became corrupted and broken whilst you indulged your every whim, uncaring about the conditions of your people.

Your *fake God Toral* did nothing to help those who were supposed to be *His* people, yet Saritin is different. Saritin does not simply speak of consequences; Saritin delivers retribution with force and vengeance. We are here today because of your actions, Emperor Jhaerin, and this boy will die because of you!"

Jhaerin could feel Panitias's eyes on him, penetrating him to the core. He could not look back, could not face looking her in the eyes and admitting that guilt. As much as it hurt him to admit it, he could not argue with this man's words.

I did fail my people. The fate they will receive will be because of me. Their blood will be on my hands.

Jhaerin's body was so numb, even tears would not come.

My boy, my beautiful boy. What have I done? How have I allowed this to happen?

Passin was trying his hardest to stop his body from shaking as he stood, fully robed and masked, in front of the three prisoners, yet he could not control the uncontrollable. His wife and child, who were meant to be the most important people in his life, stood a mere five feet from him, not knowing who he was. *What he was.* His wife was trying her hardest to look unafraid, yet he had known her for longer than anyone alive, he saw the truth behind her facade. In her eyes he saw fear and bewilderment, as she desperately looked from man to man, secretly pleading, begging for respite even in their steeliness, yet when they looked upon Passin, they had no idea of the man that stood beneath.

The monster that stands beneath!

His boy, eight years old, looked almost fearless. For all his whimpers earlier, he now stood like a man, accepting his fate, unwilling to die like a coward.
More of a man than his father.
Oh, the mistake I've made. Is there a level low enough in Saritins Chambers for a man like me? I do not deserve to be embraced by him, I deserve to be mauled, punished, the worst punishments known to man.
I have forsaken my own flesh and blood.
Lutander had been talking for some time now, mainly taunting the ex-Emperor, yet Passin could not concentrate on his words, the situation was too intense for him. Would the other men see him shaking? Would they take him for a coward? He had sacrificed too much to be forsaken at this late stage, with this much at stake. For all his regret and self hate, he knew that turning at this late stage was pointless. His family were un-savable, there was only himself left to be concerned about.
Lutander spoke. "These men you see before you are the headsmen of *Saritin,* special envoys of the *Dark Lord,* bringers of his presence on this earth. Darkness has descended, never will you see the light again. Men, unmask yourselves and show these followers of the *fake God* the faces that will see them to their deaths."
The words struck Passin hard, his knees almost buckled beneath him, and a bitter tasting bile rose in his throat.
Unmask ourselves?
The thought of seeing the look of horror and disgust in his wife's face, the look of confusion and desperation on his son's, was almost too much for Passin. He had always assumed he would keep his mask on, until Saritin showed himself anyway. He toyed with the

idea of running off, surely Lutander would understand? But would Saritin?

You've sacrificed too much to risk it. This Empire will be yours, Saritin will embrace you, and you will never again be hurt like you have been before. The simple act of taking off your mask is all that is required.

The two other Acolytes standing before the trio of prisoners had already unmasked themselves, casually displaying faces which held no recognition for the captives, cruel eyes darting over all three, sizing them up, evil plans of what they intended to do clearly being created on the whim. Passin paused, steeling himself. He could sense Lutander's eyes on him, burning through him, sizing him up.

This is a test. He is determining my commitment! I've come too far, sacrificed too much.

With a hesitant grab of a handful of the fabric atop his head, Passin pulled the mask right over his head, revealing to his family his familiar scarred face. The look in their eyes was one that would stay with him for all of eternity.

The top of the mountain had gone a ghastly quiet, no one was saying a word. From his vantage point, Saerphin was still trying to process what he had just seen. His body had gone rigid cold, his heart felt as though it had stopped, his mouth involuntarily slacked open, he was ignorant to all but what he had just seen. His eyes were zoomed in on his brother, his brain desperately asking them the same question over and over again.

Passin. My brother Passin. Can it truly be him? How can this be?

Passin's disappearance had not seemed strange to Saerphin, nor Panitias for that matter, as he often went away for days at a time. The coincidence that he

had gone at the same time as Zanati was taken did not even seem overly strange. But for this? To betray his family, worship this evil *Dark Lord?* The men he had hated for so long, his brother was one of them? And to make matters worse, had been involved in kidnapping his *own son?*
Saerphin did not want to believe it, yet at this point knew he had no choice. The evidence was in front of him, and he did not have time to be shell-shocked. His options were limited, but he had to do something. The time was now to act, without a doubt. For the first time since before he could remember, Saerphin prayed. *Please Lord, don't let Saritin be the only Godly presence upon this mountain tonight!*

Panitias's mouth was gagged tightly, preventing all words from being spoken. All she could do was stare, stare through tear soaked eyes in shock. Stare at the man who had professed his love for her, professed his devotion, professed that he would be hers forever, to protect her, to cherish her. The man who had created with her the child which stood in almost touching distance of her, the child which this man had forsaken. The child which at this moment he could not even look at, although he had not taken his eyes off her's since his unmasking.
It is not a man that stands before me. It is a monster.
Panitias could not take her eyes off her husband, the hate building within her to the point she felt it would explode from within, releasing a torrent of vile, putrid substance, so vicious it would burn her husband alive, allow her to unleash herself from her captivity and extract the vengeance on this man he so thoroughly deserved. The darkest corners of Saritins Chambers were reserved for the type of evil Passin had

committed, she could only hope they were wrong about Saritin's presence here tonight.

With Toral as my witness, if I have to kill Saritin himself here tonight to get retribution, that is what I will do. My husband shall not get away with this.

The leader seemed to be enjoying himself, a contented smirk overpowered his aged face as he glanced from Passin to Panitias, and back again, his head moving backwards and forwards like he was watching a dual. "Your own husband, who would have thought it? And you, little man?" The old man was looking straight at Zanati, whose bravery had deserted him the second he saw his father standing before him, and who was now whimpering uncontrollably, a muffled squeak all that could be heard through the gag, his eyes wide and confused.

"Did you have any idea your daddy was the reason you were here today? It was all his idea." The condescending tone of this depraved man's voice was torturous to Panitias.

He's enjoying this, my life has been ripped from me and he's enjoying it.

At that moment Panitias did not know whose body she wanted ripped from limb to limb more, the old man's or her husbands, but her perspective was soon back in place and she knew who the real enemy here was. All she wanted to do was ask him why? Why he had forsaken his child, his wife, why he had chosen these men over his family? What had she done, what had Zanati done, which had made him so bitter, capable of such evil? He had not spoke one word since his mask had been removed, could he not answer that one question?

Without warning, sudden movements whizzed in every direction, and Acolytes began falling. The sound of men crying out in pain was all around, half terrifying and half elating for Panitias. It did not take her long to realize the whizzing movements were arrows, being distributed from the back end of the mountain. As she looked in that direction, she could see several burly men running to their opponents, ready to commence battle. She knew the serpent tattoos well, and had never been so happy to see Serintinals in her life.

Ajinaxa was one of the first to launch the assault, always prepared to lead from the front, guide his men into battle and risk all. The climb had been dangerous, two men climbing unaided up the vertical cliff then securing ropes for those below, but it had been worthwhile in ensuring the effect of surprise. These men had not seen them coming, and were now scampering around confused, unsure who their enemy was or where they were coming from. It was even worth the cost of the three men who had fallen to their deaths mid climb, a fate which had almost been that of Ajinaxa.

Terrifying, but far from the worst way to get your adrenaline pumping. Ajinaxa felt as though he could face all the Acolytes present on his own, such was his jubilation at surviving the climb.

Ajinaxa reached the first Acolyte, his steel clashing heavily with the man's shield, but an opening formed from the collision enabled him to force his sword through, inserting it viciously through the man's eye socket, crashing through his skull and out the other side, a sickening split heard as steel ripped bone to pieces. Another man came rushing to him from his left, sword aloft, and for a second Ajinaxa realized the danger he was in, his sword stubbornly stuck in the first man's head, unmoving. Luckily for him, one of his men was just behind, and as the Acolyte raised his

sword to strike, drove his blade right through the man's chest, perforating whichever organs got in the way and drawing a stream of thick blood gushing from the man's mouth before he collapsed to the floor.
Ajinaxa gave his savior a look of gratitude, before powerfully forcing his sword through bone and brain to its release and continuing to his next opponent. The sound of swords clashing, the shriek of pain, the adrenaline rushing through his body. This was what life was about for Ajinaxa, he could live this moment forever.

Saerphin had seen the commotion and acted on instinct. His original plan had been suicidal, borne of a lack of realistic options, but now he knew he stood a chance.
Keeping his eyes firmly planted on the location of his Nephew and Sister-in-Law, Saerphin hopped from the tree, his feet slipping on the wet grass so he was on his knees in seconds. The rain was gradually getting stronger, impairing his vision, but he knew where he needed to be. He got up and began moving expertly towards his targets. The wind atop the mountain would have made him cold, if it were not for the surge of adrenaline which had overtaken him.
I stand a chance; I can get my Nephew back. Sweet Zanati.
Two Acolytes were standing facing the position of their assaulters, completely unaware of Saerphin's presence a mere five foot behind them. With an agile, cat like movement he wrapped his blade around the first man's throat and sliced efficiently, the familiar sound of air escaping the man's throat where words would no longer was like music to Saerphin's ears. Before the second man could properly react, Saerphin was upon him, a back arm slash with Xinias catching

the man across the chest, the razor sharp blade skimming through chest muscles before penetrating his heart, sending the man crashing to his death.

This is more like it. This is what I know. This is who I am.

Looking around, all Saerphin could see was chaos, a sea of red masks and serpent tattoos, blood and death everywhere, pain and suffering, victory and defeat. To calculate which side was winning, or even how many men were on each side, would have been impossible, the men from both sides seem to merge into a twisted collage of destruction, red masks, serpent tattoos, blood and chaos.

Looking to his left, Saerphin could see his Nephew and his Sister-in-Law, Panitias on her knees embracing the boy tightly, tears gushing from her eyes. As he started to move towards them, something else caught his eye. Passin. His brother was currently in the corner of the mountain top, shying away from the fighting, looking frightened and alone.

A coward until the end. Not fit to bear the name Barina. Saerphin knew his priority should be saving his relatives, taking them away from this place whilst everyone else was distracted with the battle, but he could not bring himself to do that. What his brother had done was unforgiveable, and on this day Saerphin intended to be judge and executioner, as he should have been all those years ago. As he began marching towards his sibling, Passin's eyes caught his, the look of terror within them was the first pleasure Saerphin had felt all day.

We've done it. Thank the Great Lord Toral, our savior, he heard our prayers, we've done it.

The sandy beaches of Atlantis were a mere few hundred yards, Gurain could not believe it. They felt almost close enough to touch.

"We're here, we've finally made it." Janithia was excited beyond being able to control himself, and throwing all caution to the wind leapt from the ship's hull into the wind swept ocean below, clearly intent on swimming the rest of the way, too eager to await the ship's journey like everyone else.

"What in the name of Atlantis did that idiot just do?" Cronias bellowed. "He better be a good swimmer if he's gonna reach shore from there in this weather."

Gurain shared the captain's worry, although he doubted the captain's concerns were for Janithias wellbeing and probably more for not wanting to lose another man. They had already lost too many men, and ships, during this ill fated conquest.

The rain was coming down without respite, and seemed to be getting heavier and heavier, to the point Gurain had to squint his eyes to see anything. Looking overboard, he could not even see whether Janithia had reemerged from below the waves. He had always told the boy that one day his impetuousness would be his downfall, although he had never thought it would be like this.

"Keep rowing, and don't any of you think of following that idiot overboard. If he survives he'll wish the waves had taken him when I get hold of him." Cronias was clearly in no mood to be trifled with. Gurain wondered whether the man was dreading having to give the news of their failure to Emperor Jhaerin and his advisors, although he knew the man would never admit such fear. He would nose dive off the ship himself before he succumbed to that.

It did not take long for them to reach shore, the ships massive hull colliding with sand before wedging in and securing itself on the beach. It had been decided the beach was a safer bet for a quick departure than any of the Empire's docks, which would have required a careful and slow stopping process involving the ships anchor to prevent the ship from destroying their landing base. The ship had not been stopped for more than a few moments before ropes secured to the mast were thrown down to the sandy beach below, and men began clambering over one another to be the first to descend.

Gurain had been near the back of the ship, and so was one of the last to the ropes. Before he descended he took one last look behind at the Greek ships, barely visible but for their torches. He did not know whether it was to his relief or not that they were not following, but instead seemed content to sit and wait. The wind blew heavily on him as he climbed down the rope.

My plan, my plan, what's happened to my plan?

Lutander was stood in the middle of the action, yet no one looked at him twice. *The kind looking old man must be caught up in this involuntarily, probably a hostage,* these Serintinals must be thinking.

I am the reason we are here today. I am the man to bring Saritin to this Empire tonight, and even with these men's presence, He will come. I will not be foiled in this, He will come!

Lutander had worked too hard, had perfected this plan too greatly, in too much detail, to allow anything to stop him.

As he looked around him, all he saw were mounds of dead Acolytes, from what he could tell almost double that of the Serintinals. He was not surprised. *Trained soldiers against citizens, men whose greatest weapon was their zealotry, whose faith in the True God, the Dark Lord Saritin had brought them here tonight,*

brought them to their slaughter. Will the Dark Lord see their true devotion to him through their actions and embrace them still? If I were to fall, would he embrace me?
The thought scared Lutander.
He could not allow that to happen. He would not die a mortal tonight, he would become a God, a demon who would answer to no one but Saritin himself. He had planned too greatly to allow anything but that to happen.
The boy. The idea struck him like lightning. The boy was still here, the boy's death was the act which would show their true devotion to *Saritin* and bring about his presence on this earth. *If the boy dies, Saritin comes.*
Looking around, his vision difficult due to the now heavy rain, Lutander finally saw what he was looking for. In the corner, alongside his tearful mother and the crippled ex-Emperor, was the boy. Lutander did not take his steely gaze off him as he marched purposely in his direction, ready to kill with any means at his disposal.

Ajinaxa was now heavily in the midst of the battle, his brow covered with a thick sweat, his hands and tunic transformed from white to a dark crimson. Some of the blood was his own, although in his state of frenzy he did not feel any pain from his wounds. Most of the blood belonged to others though, slain men who posed him no more threat due to the damage his sword had imposed on them.
A large set man with narrow eyes rushed towards him from a few yards to his left, Ajinaxa ducked the man's wild swing and sliced his sword brutally across the man's belly, before leaving him behind to die a painful death, his cries almost inhuman. Another man tried a

similar move, this time from the right, at least this time Ajinaxa had to work for his kill, skillfully parrying the blow before powerfully driving his sword through the man's throat, the gushing blood adding further crimson to Ajinaxas tunic. All Ajinaxa could hear was chaos, all he could smell was blood and death. All he could see was chaos, except for in one corner of the mountain top, not far from his current location. Amidst the battle and chaos something was out of place. Ajinaxa stopped and stared, unsure if his eyes were betraying him or if he was really seeing who he thought he was seeing.
Prization.
The man with no soul.
 Ajinaxa knew exactly who the large man lethargically strolling around the edge of the battle was. He had never met him, but one look was all he needed. The man's size, his soulless eyes, the way he was carelessly wandering around the battle, as though he thought battles with lesser men such as these were below him. Prization had his eyes set on the big man and could not take them off, even if he had wanted to. Steeling himself, he approached. He knew the danger the big man imposed, and he knew the importance of what he had to do. He was determined this was the one fight where the legendary Prization would not emerge victor.

Prization looked at Ajinaxa, past him at first but there was something that made him look back at the burly man approaching. The other Serintinals had seemingly been doing all they could to avoid Prization, and the general area he was in. Men tended to do that when they saw him, even if they did not know who he was or the acts he had committed in his life. Prization knew he was different to most men, that there was something about him that made men wary, intimidated.

But this man was different, Prization could see a steely look in his eyes, a dogged determination. He did not know who this man was, but that was irrelevant. This was what he had been waiting for all night.

As Ajinaxa approached, he could see the big man's eyes were directly on him now, searing through his flesh and bone.

No turning back now.

It was ironic that a man with such soulless eyes could stare at a man in such a way that it seemed as though he was staring straight into their soul. Ajinaxa did not flinch, did not waver, and did not give any indication of fear to this revered warrior. He knew the psychology of battle well enough to know the advantage he would give the man if he showed any weakness, and he knew the cost of giving Prization that advantage. No amount of fear could allow Ajinaxa to revert from his fearless face, he could not allow his mind to betray his body.

Ajinaxa walked to within ten yards of Prization then stopped, eyeing up his opponent, weighing his strengths, trying to identify his weaknesses. The two men did not blink, did not twitch. They both knew the first to look away had given the other a huge advantage, and remained defiantly staring as such. No words were needed, both men knew what was about to happen.

Eventually, Prization was the first to blink, before grabbing the handle of his monstrous blade and slowly unsheathing it. The steely look in his eyes told Ajinaxa he may have lost the battle, but that Prization was still confident of winning the war. This was not a man who lost often, if he ever had, and he did not intend on that changing today

The dance began. Prization took a long stride forward, sword extended, Ajinaxa took a step to the right. Prization brought his sword into a striking pose, Ajinaxa did the same. Both men were waiting on the other, silently urging them to strike first, so that they could counter the blow and land some damage on their opponent. Neither man was willing to be the first to strike, this had become a war of attrition.
Out of the corner of his eyes, Ajinaxa could see the battles going on around him. He could not tell who was winning and who was losing, who was being killed as he played his game of patience with the big man, and that was when he realized he was at a disadvantage. Prization had all the time in the world, he probably had already been paid and did not care less whether every Acolyte atop the mountain was slain, such was his arrogance that he no doubt believed that he could kill every remaining Serintinel afterwards. Ajinaxa did not have that luxury. He had to try and win as fast as possible, to help his men, to accomplish what he had come here to do.
The thought had distracted Ajinaxa for a moment too long, before he could react he saw Prizations enormous blade heading straight for his neck.

The two brothers were now but a few feet away from each other, face to face, man to man.
Man to coward, thought Passin. Since the moment he had been tasked by Lutander with this evil, this was the moment he had dreaded, the moment that had dominated his dreams and infiltrated his nightmares. He had pictured the confrontation in a thousand different ways, but this had not been one of them. The

boy still alive, the plan all but dead, his brothers being slaughtered all around him like animals. For all his disappointment, he did not expect one ounce of pity from his brother, he knew what was coming. He *deserved* what was coming.

"Why." Saerphin asked. One simple word, so many different answers, each one complex, each one irrelevant. Why did not matter, why was based around what had been done, all that was pertinent now was what was to be done. He had been willing to sacrifice his own child, was his brother capable of slaying his own kin also?

"I am not going to stand before you and explain why I did what I did, Saerphin. I don't even know if I can. All I can say is, I know what you have to do, and I understand it." Passin's voice was soft, regretful. He knew his brother well enough to know he would require more than that to stand a chance of mercy. Saerphin's moral compass, his sense of decency and justice, was greater than that of any man Passin had met.

"You're right on one thing at least, you can't explain why you did it. No reason possible can be good enough for what you have done, and no punishment can be too severe. As much as it pains me to be the bringer of justice to my own kin, I cannot allow you to walk away today." Saerphin raised Xinias to Passin's throat, the tip of the blade balanced just under his chin. "Kneel."

Passin obeyed, lowering himself onto both knees, his whole body shaking violently.

"Your *Dark Lord* cannot save you now brother, I pray to *Toral* the souls of mother and father can at least bring themselves to forgive you for your actions. I will never be able to."

Saerphin raised his sword high, ready to strike the killer blow.

"Saerphin, help!" Panitias was screaming at the top of her lungs, the noise carried throughout the mountain top. It only took Saerphin to look away for a second for Passin to seize the opportunity, and before Saerphin could bring his blade back to his brother he was gone, scrambling across the mountain and to the sanctity of several of his Acolyte brothers, those who were still fighting on.

I'll get him later. Looking over towards where Panitias had been screaming from, Saerphin could see he now had greater priorities. Lutander had Zanati by his collar, and was edging him close to the edge of the mountain, threatening to throw him over if everyone did not back up from him.

If he goes over the edge, you'll be following him, Saerphin thought as he began his sprint over to his ailing Nephew.

"Back up, or the boy goes over the edge!" Lutander was threatening. He was surrounded by enemies, most of his Acolytes dead, and was without doubt to anyone now a very desperate man, his plan unveiled, his future destroyed. The boy's death was his last hope of salvation.

Saritin don't fail me now.

"The boy goes over the edge, you follow him." The voice was familiar to Lutander, although he doubted its owner remembered who he was. Lutander, or Avyon as the man would have known him as, had heard Saerphin Barina speak at more Palace meetings than he could remember, but only once had they spoken together, over some trivial matter. But despite their lack of intimacy, Lutander knew exactly what Saerphin was capable of, and did not doubt the sincerity of his words.

"You come any nearer, and the boy goes over. I came here today prepared to die, all in the name of the *True God,* the *Dark Lord Saritin,* whose rising will see you all condemned. It's not too late, vow your allegiance and you will all be embraced by *Him,* made allies and given glorious lives, lives of luxury, in his embrace. All that has to happen is this *one child* has to die."

Zanati had not stopped squirming since Lutander had grabbed him, causing Lutander to dig his nails deeper and deeper into the child's shoulders to secure his grip. The mention of him dying caused his sobs to increase, much to Lutander's annoyance.

"Put the child down Lutander, and walk away, we can find a way out of this."

Lutander was stunned, as he spun his head around to the left and saw the speaker of those words. "Passin, what are you talking of? You're as much a part of this as me. We've come too far, there's no turning back now. The boy *has* to die, it's all part of the plan."

Passin could feel eyes from every direction staring directly at him, all laced with hate and malice. He did not doubt he deserved it, although he doubted anyone present hated him more than he hated himself at that moment.

"We've made a mistake, it's not going to happen tonight. If you fall with the child, then what? Will Saritin come? There is no one left for him to embrace. You will be dead, I will be dead. I do not want my child dying for nothing."

Without being able to control herself any longer, Panitias marched to her husband and exerted every ounce of power she possessed to deliver a stinging slap across his face, the connection heard across the mountain.

"Zanati is your son, you monster. You shouldn't want him to die for any reason. You're meant to be the one protecting him, yet you've brought him to be sacrificed, like an animal. I don't know who you are, but you are not the man I married."

Passin was speechless, unable to respond. His brother's presence at the end, he had always known was a strong possibility, but he had never expected to have to face his wife, with her knowing what he had done.

"All I want to know is why?" Panitias continued, her voice breaking as she spoke.

That question again, why? All eyes were on the two of them, husband and wife, a very public domestic argument which seemed to have caught the attention of all, everyone eager for an answer off Passin, willing to put what they were doing on hold to receive one.

"I…I wish I had an answer. I was hurt and lonely when Zarias died, and my brothers took me in. They turned my sorrow to a purpose, and made me realize who the *True* God is. Saritin would not have allowed what *Toral* did if I had placed my trust and prayers in him. I saw the error in my ways, and vowed to never fight for the wrong side again."

"Never fight for the wrong side again? You've tried to sacrifice your son, your flesh and blood, for your so called *brothers.* What type of man does that?"

Passin sighed, trying to find an answer that would justify his actions, although very aware that one did not exist. "When Zarias died I was devastated. He was to be the greatest man the Empire had ever seen, greater than even my brother." Passin glanced at Saerphin quickly, but received only a look of hatred back. "For the chance to be embraced by *Saritin,* to be taken in to his Chambers and join *His* uprising, I was willing to sacrifice my only living child, because my only living child was expendable. He was not Zarias, never had his promise, his strength, his character. I never...I never loved Zanati in the way I loved Zarias."

The words sent shockwaves through Panitias, shaking her to her core.

"You never loved Zanati? What type of man says that?" She looked at her baby, scared and confused, held tightly by an evil man threatening to end his life at any moment, and wondered how any father could not love their child.

"He was not the chosen one, the greatest man the Empire had ever seen. *Toral* allowed that child to be taken from me, I could never understand why."

"He wasn't." Panitias retorted.

Passin took a step back in shock. "What do you mean?"

"The child who the prophet said would be the 'greatest man that ever lived in Atlantis.' He wasn't taken from you." Despite the situation, Panitias enjoyed the look of confusion and shock on her husband's face. She knew it may be the only victory she had over him that day.

"What do you mean, he wasn't taken from me? I was there when he was taken, devoured by animals like he was prey. They took him, I knew they did."

"I lied when I said the prophet said our first born would be 'the greatest man the Empire had ever seen.' Zarias had been born, but I was not sure I could conceive another, was not sure I even wanted another mouth to feed. Times were hard. So I told you our first child was who the prophet was speaking of. He was not. The prophet predicted that....our second child, would be 'the greatest man the Empire had ever seen.'"

Passin tried processing the words, but could not, his thoughts whirling around his head in a thousand different directions at once, colliding, bouncing, infusing together until his head felt like it would implode. He stared at his only living son, confused, afraid, mortified at what he had done.

"You're lying, why wouldn't you have told me sooner?"

"Why would I have? Do you think I ever suspected that just because he wasn't prophesised as a legend that you wouldn't love our son? That you would be willing to allow him to die so *you* could prosper? I had truly forgotten all about that prophecy, did not even know you remembered it. Did you truly believe in the words of some prophet? Enough to do....this?" Panitias stared at her child with sorrow. "Now that the child is important enough for you, why don't you help us? Convince this man to step away from the ledge and give us back our child."

Lutander began to laugh, a loud hearty chuckle which took everyone by surprise.

"So, as I have said all along, this boy I hold, he's prophesized to be the greatest man the Empire has ever seen? How did you not see that Passin, why do you think Saritin wanted his sacrifice so badly? I always questioned your loyalty to our cause, doubted your use, now I see what you have brought us. This boy was chosen by *Toral,* but he will die at the behest of *Saritin.* And he will die at my hands, it's perfect."

With a firm shove, before anyone could react, Lutander pushed Zanati towards the edge of the cliff, causing him to trip and stumble on the rocks just above, falling onto his side, rolling rapidly towards the edge, arms stuck underneath him with each roll, desperately trying to grab anything to break his fall.

Jhaerin was the first to react, and the closest. As Zanati began to roll over the edge of the cliff, Jhaerin jumped to the boy, hand stretched out to be grabbed, desperate to save the child from his impending fate. Zanati stretched and reached for the ex-Emperor's hand to halt his fall....the boy's fingers touched the old mans skin....before his fingertips brushed the stump where the old mans hand had once been. With nothing to stop his fall, the child fell, spiraling downwards, his screaming heard by all, piercing, sickening, until he had fallen so far his screams could be heard no more. They did not need to hear the thud he made as he struck the jagged rocks below to know the boy was dead.
A monstrous crackle of thunder roared overhead.

Everyone present had rushed to the edge of the cliff to look below, hope in their hearts that some miracle would halt Zanati's fall, some tree protruding from the mountain, some rock, perhaps *Toral* himself grabbing him out of thin air. The heavy rain and wind made seeing below difficult, but they all knew the truth, their prayers had not been answered.
My child. He was to be the true greatest man alive, and I sacrificed him. I allowed this to happen. I brought this evil into the world.
The pain that had overtaken Passin was far too great to bear, he felt as though his heart were about to explode. He would have welcomed it, to put an end to the pain, but it did not come. He was responsible for his son's death, and would have to pay the consequences.
For once in my life, I will pay the price for my actions.
Without a word, without a final prayer, without even looking at his wife one more time, Passin jumped blindly from the mountain, his arms outstretched,

embracing his fate, the fate his son had faced because of him. For a few long moments the swirling wind held him, made him feel like he was flying, he felt more alive than he had felt in a long time. Then he felt nothing.

Jhaerin was still laid on his front, outstretched arm perched just over the edge of the mountain. He could not stop staring at his hand, or more accurately the stump where his hand had once been. The stump where, if his hand still was, the child would still be alive, embracing his mother even now. The Empire might still have a chance of survival, his people may be allowed to live. As it was, he looked up towards the wails which were coming from the mother. This was the hardest thing he had ever had to hear.

Why did I do it? I could have done anything to punish myself, why my hand? Why that hand? Why did I offer that hand for help? Why was I not faster? Why did I allow this Empire to become so corrupted, so distorted in its morals that this was allowed to happen in the first place? Where was I when these men were given free range to created havoc like this? Why were they allowed to prosper within my Empire?

Jhaerin could not answer any of the questions, all he could do was lie in the mud and stare at his stump. The punishment he had afforded himself where he could have done anything had cost the entire Empire everything.

I did it. I did it. The boy is dead, I'm going to be a God! A true God, powerful over all.

Everyone had been distracted by the boy, and were now too shocked to move. They did not keep track of Lutander creeping away, and by now he had made his way across the mountain top, under the cover of several trees to the sea side of the mountain.

When will Saritin come for me? Will he appear from nowhere, as though a magician, and smite these non-believers? Lutander could not wait, the suspense was painful in itself.

All around him battles were still raging, although there were but a few Acolytes left, the clever ones who had ganged together and holed themselves into positions which were difficult to get to. He was pleased to see, calculating the numbers dead and the number still fighting, that it did not appear many, if any of his men had deserted. They knew the cost of turning their backs on Saritin, and would be rewarded greatly for their loyalty. The numbers the men still fighting were facing were insurmountable, but the outcome was irrelevant.

Out of the corner of his eye Lutander noticed Prization, the large mercenary whose services he had acquired at great cost. Gazing upon the man mid combat, Lutander could see that the cost was for nothing. Five men surrounded the giant, as he swung at one man, another swiped at him from behind. The Serintinals seemed to be enjoying the game, they clearly knew who the big man was, and with every swing he got more and more tired. Eventually, the Serintinals tired of the game as well, and with his back turned to him one of them sliced his sword across Prizations right knee, bringing the big man to the floor face first, and all five Serintinals proceeded to pounce, mercilessly delivering a frenzied barrage of stabs to every part of Prizations body, devouring him, leaving nothing to chance and enjoying themselves in the process.

The less Acolytes when Saritin ascends upon us, the more praise for me. The true survivor, who could not be smitten by these mortal warriors. Their mortality will be proven when Saritin arrives, and smites every last one of them.

Lutander thought he saw something, a flash in front of him.

That must be him!

But nothing immortal came, just a flash of lightning which crashed atop the mountain, dangerously close. The storm was becoming ferocious, battering against the mountain. The wind was becoming so great that it would soon be strong enough to blow grown men over the mountain side, to share Zanati's fate, and the thunder and lightning was becoming more and more frequent. In the past few moments the rains intensity had quickened rapidly.

Good. Dark weather for dark deeds, Saritin will appreciate what I have given him.

But where is He?

Lutander looked across the mountain top, to the sea, and noticed something he had not noticed before. As the storm got stronger, and the rain became heavier, so heavy now its force was almost enough to knock him from his feet, the waters were rising. *How could that be? Is this the work of Saritin? Is this his way of smiting the weak?*

Lutander did not have long to think about it. He did not see Saerphin behind him, the first knowledge he had of his presence was when the ex-Serintinal pressed his cold blade to his throat, so tightly it drew blood.

"Your time's up, old man." He growled. "Come with me, I know someone who can't wait to get their hands on you."

34

Morning must have come by now, but there was no way to tell. The rain and thunder clouds were preventing all light from emerging, casting the entire Empire in an eerie darkness which made the flash floods that had cascaded continuously upon the Empire even more dangerous. The people had never seen rain like this before, and in their droves they had begun searching for higher ground, their homes and livelihoods destroyed, their families being plucked from them as they moved, the weakest most vulnerable to the heavy rains, their families mostly unable to save them.

However heartbreaking it was, most of the families knew once a loved one was stolen from them by the waters irresistible current there was nothing to be done for them, and that they had to continue on their desperate search for salvation, accept that their loved ones had been taken by *The Great Lord Toral*. A few could not accept this fate for their loved ones. Husbands searched desperately up newly formed rivers for wives, mothers for children, children for parents. The results were always the same, the inhuman cries of anguish mostly drowned by the irrepressible lashing of rain, deafening even in its rare quieter spells.

The scores of bodies floating within the newly imposed rivers flowing through the villages all around Jhaerin said all that needed to be told of the dangers created by the heavy flowing water, and the abruptness in which the water had infiltrated the homes of the local people had taken all by surprise.

It has begun, and it will soon be over. There is no saving us, not now. Our chance for repentance has passed.

Jhaerin had been advised to stay atop the mountain, but had declined the advice. He knew what was coming, had seen it every time he had closed his eyes, ever since that dream. He knew there was no escaping it, the unrelenting chaos and wanton destruction, endless deaths, the water extinguishing the flames of the soul of the Empire, bringing upon them eternal darkness.

All my fault.

Jhaerin knew he deserved any punishment afforded him, yet those up the mountain had been anything but scornful, instead embracing him, trying to absolve him of responsibility, assuring him that the evil was that of others, not himself. In a lot of ways, their kindness hurt more than if they had thrown him from the mountain.

There are still good people in this Empire, and I have brought this fate upon them. The Great Lord Toral sees to punish them for my weakness.

He had prayed they would throw him from the mountain, or end his life in any way, so that he would not need to see what was now in front of him, what he knew was coming. But they had not. This was his destruction to see; he would not be saved from the images in front of him.

The guilt of his actions was half of what constrained his mind, the other half was his son.

Where are you now? Are you scared? Are you alone? Do you need your father? Do you wonder where he is? Do you hate me, or is there still love in your heart?

Seeing Zanati thrown from the mountain had broken Jhaerin's heart, seeing a child so promising destroyed by a man so evil. All he could think of was *what if that had been Tinithius? Would my son die thinking that I did not love him? That I had abandoned him?* It was painfully ironic that abdication had been the most selfless act that Jhaerin had ever committed, yet in his son's eyes it must have seemed like the most selfish act on earth.

I acted for the good of my people...for the good of your people...I pray to Toral you see that my child. I will beg for your forgiveness in the next life, should Toral see fit to place us together. I will pray that he does.

The anger Jhaerin had felt at Avyon had been visceral and uncompromising, the same as every other body still breathing upon that mountain. A mother had lost her only living child, taken for the most evil of reasons, and for that no man could be forgiven. Lutander still seemed to hold to the notion that *Saritin* would appear from nowhere, to smite his enemies and deliver him his prize. The only memory of the previous night that brought any joy to Jhaerin was the last he had seen of Lutander, tied naked to a tree, facing the sea, left at the mercy of the cold and the elements. Jhaerin doubted the man was still alive, and if he was he probably did not want to be anymore. Never before had he wished such pain upon another human being, nor enjoyed another man's pain so much.

Was that really the same Avyon the priests called Grandfather?

From his vantage point upon a nearby hillside, Jhaerin could see for miles around. He could see the Palace, where his son had been, where he had ruled for so many years. But his son was there no more, apparently taken to higher ground earlier that morning. Jhaerin had travelled here to be with his son, yet for his evil this was to be his final punishment.

I came back to you; I did. I came back to beg your forgiveness, to be together in our final moments. They took you to higher ground but soon there will be no higher ground. For what I've done you will suffer the same fate as the rest of the Empire. You, my son, were always stronger than me. You must be strong now.

Jhaerin would have given anything to see his son's face, to say his apologies and explain his actions. But it was too late; he would never have the chance again.

Dark clouds for dark deeds indeed. When Jhaerin's grandmother used to say that, he never thought he would ever see weather this dark.

Jhaerin glanced to his left, he had been so engrossed in his own thoughts that he had not realized he had been joined by another. He could barely see the man through the lashing rain, but without a doubt there was another man there, a mere three foot from where he was sitting. Both men were sitting atop the mountain, trying to see what was left of the City of Pariass, of the Empire of Atlantis. All that could be seen were several high mountains in the distance, and waves, fearsome waves which with every passing moment were coming closer and closer, higher and higher, ever nearer to ascending over the mountain and ending Jhaerin's pain.

The newcomer smiled at Jhaerin, a genuine smile. He seemed unafraid, almost content. Through the noise of the rain he yelled. "I sailed a thousand miles to come here. I put every last strain of energy in my body to return home, to save my family from our enemies, yet I come home to find that our foreign enemies were not our greatest threat." The man sighed. "I rowed past the point I had thought any man capable, put my body past a pain threshold which I was sure would make me pass out, and this is my reward. I return to find my village flooded, my family dead. What God would allow this?"

Jhaerin looked at the man for a long moment, a thousand thoughts running through his head, yet feeling more at peace than he had in a long time. "My brother, it is us who are to blame for your loss, not our God. Our Empire which has spat in the face of *Toral* for so long is now facing the consequences. I am very sorry for your loss, but I can assure you, your pain will be but fleeting. I pray that you find peace in the next life."

The man did not reply; his eyes were now focused on the waves that were by now just below them both. He looked as though he was almost pleading with them to hurry up, to come take him and end his pain.

Looking around at the death and destruction which had overrun this once great Empire, Jhaerin allowed himself the luxury of one last fleeting memory, reminiscing of a time when the lands were green and lush, the Empire overflowing with promise and beauty, the people happy, the *one true God* content. The memory was of a long time ago, and passed in the wind with the same speed that the time itself seemed to have gone, stolen, never to be returned.

A steely bravery overcame the ex-Emperor. Staring his impending death in the eye, it took all Jhaerin's strength to force himself to his feet, bracing himself, ready for anything. He could not have prepared himself for the sensation of helplessness as the wave crashed upon him, plucking him from the Empire he had loved like a mother plucking her baby from their basket. As the descending wave crashed over him, lifting him up, taking his breath, filling his lungs with a never ending torrent of salty punishment, he had never felt so at peace in his life.

Printed in Great Britain
by Amazon.co.uk, Ltd.,
Marston Gate.